Praise for *Tushpa's Story*

Tushpa's Story was a wonderful read. Sarah Elisabeth did a wonderful job portraying the heart and spirit of the Choctaw people during this time of our history. I can't wait to read what she comes up with next!

Ryan L. Spring, Historic Preservation Department
Choctaw Nation of Oklahoma

As a great-granddaughter of Tushpa, a boy on the Trail of Tears, I grew up far away from Oklahoma with little knowledge of our history. It is through reading the moving stories collected here by Sarah Elisabeth Sawyer that I have a better understanding of the struggles, endurance and bravery of our Choctaw ancestors.

Beverly Bringle, direct descendant of Tushpa

Wow. Several parts actually led me to tears.

Francine Locke Bray, Choctaw historian

Tushpa's Story

A Novella

Touch My Tears: Tales from the Trail of Tears Collection

SARAH ELISABETH SAWYER

ROCKHAVEN PUBLISHING

RockHaven Publishing
P.O. Box 1103
Canton, Texas 75103

Editors: Lynda Kay Sawyer, James Masters

Interior Design: Sarah Elisabeth Sawyer

Cover Design: Kirk DouPonce (www.DogEaredDesign.com)

Author Photo by R. A. Whiteside. Courtesy of the National Museum of the American Indian, Smithsonian Institution

ISBN: 0-9910259-3-8
ISBN-13: 978-0-9910259-3-0
LCCN: 2016930620

For Beverly Bringle
and
Marilou Awiakta
Yakoke

"All of this I have faithfully performed as I write this tribute to his memory that others may know and become such as he was by the grace of God." —James Culberson

Chapter One

Who died? The question beat in my mind in rhythm to my steps as I walked with my mother and father to the burial grounds. No word had circulated of a loved one's death among the dozens of Chahta families as we all prepared to march hundreds of miles to a new land. But it seemed necessary to the older ones that they make a visit to the place where the bones of our relatives rested.

My father, Kanchi, led the way as families joined us in the slow walk to the burial grounds. My father was a head taller than most Chahta men. I never walked too close to him because I wanted to be able to see his face without falling over backwards. He had a sharp face, his jawline distinct and definite. I felt small next to him, not quite the height of his chest. I did share his dark brown eyes and long, loose black hair.

More and more walked alongside us now, until the entire band had joined together as one. And one we must become to survive, my father said.

Finally, the grave houses came into sight, little log structures covering the resting places of my ancestors. I glanced around for a new grave house, the one we'd come to mourn at. But instead, the eldest ones of the group—along with our head chief, Baha—formed the inner circle in the midst of the resting place.

Chief wore a red turban wrapped around his folded black hair, the kind of blue-black of a crow's feathers when light wasn't shining on it. But sunlight showed the traces of white coming from beneath the turban. His turquoise hunting coat—made from the trade cloth brought by French explorers long ago—fit loosely over his boulder frame. His round cheeks almost met the wide white collar of his shirt, and did touch when Chief turned his head to look around. And he was always turning his head, always looking, always watching over our people.

My father joined the second circle and I found myself in the outer one between my friend Ishtaya and my mother. Ishtaya was my height, though not as fast when we ran barefoot through the woods. His black hair hung over his bony shoulders, and brushed the russet skin of his face when he turned to look at me.

We boys were not yet at manhood, but we imitated our fathers in front of us, standing tall and somber. My father was tallest in the circle, easy to see. A leather pouch hung around his neck, something bulging inside.

Chief Baha began, and as impossible as it seemed, everything around us fell into greater silence. "We have gathered here as a people many times to have a *yaya*, a cry of remembrance when we lost a loved one. Now we gather to relieve another kind of grief, the loss of our homeland. To say goodbye to a land which we will see no more."

Someone moaned, one of such pain that to hold it in would cause a heart to burst. A wail went up from the inner circle, and an old woman cried, "We are a lost people. A lost people."

I bowed my head, not strictly from respect, but with thoughts racing. One by one, each person in the circles before me spoke of the good of our homeland, withholding any evil from their speech. What would I say when my turn came? We were leaving a land we loved. How was a boy to understand so much in so little time? I feared to speak in front of everyone.

We hadn't brought food as was customary for a yaya, and I rubbed my stomach to silence its growl. Something important was taking place in this moment. How could I think of food now? Still, the growling and hunger pangs went on. And the fear.

My attention peaked when my father lifted his hands and parted his lips, but no words came out. I held my breath. Though my father kept silent much of the time at gatherings, surely he would not fail to say something to bring honor to us all. But my father said nothing and, after a time, dropped his hands to his sides.

A river of words continued round the circle; no one rushed in saying their parting words. My mother spoke hers quietly, and the group stood motionless to hear her grief. Her simple but sure ways made those around her pay attention when she spoke or acted.

My mother was a beautiful woman. Even when sad, her eyes were soft and knowing. Like the other women, she wore a simple dress but she'd adorned it with a beaded diamond design around her neckline.

When she fell silent, I sensed every face turn toward me. Even my friend Ishtaya turned slightly, as if wanting direction on what he might say.

I pulled my head between my thin shoulders like a *luksi*, a turtle. Something as sacred as this moment deserved great words, but if my own father could not give them, how could I?

Finally, I mumbled in a squeaky voice just loud enough to be heard by a few, "*Chi hullo li*. I love you."

Nothing noteworthy, nothing deserving of the nods around the circles. Ishtaya commended with, "*Ome*."

The time for the cry ended.

After hastened preparations, my parents and I were among the first families to arrive at the Great River. As temporary camp construction began, I joined my father, Kanchi, Chief Baha and second chief, Halbi, who stood on a fallen tree near the angry water's edge. I listened silently to their words.

Chief pointed to the center of the river. "That is *Bihi* Island. In my many crossings to visit our brothers over the river, I have learned all the currents and landing places. That is the place to rest and straighten the cargo if needed. It will be an easy crossing, but we must prepare."

I studied the face of the chief. Though far from old age, his skin was worn from years of travel and responsibility for his people. But even in this crisis, he took care in wearing his red turban neat around his folded hair.

The crossing was at the mouth of Cypress Creek, just south of Friars Point on this, the Mississippi River. The river stretched a mile wide. The current was stiff. But since the river was wider at the mouth of the creek, the waters calmed a bit.

Halbi motioned to the foam along the bank. "Water is high."

Our second chief always looked straight ahead, prepared to go through or over whatever stood in the way of doing what needed to be done. He was a hearty man with a square jaw and forehead, his face a burnished red from many seasons in the sun, farming his crops or hunting game to provide for his family. His wide shoulders matched the river we now faced. But looking between them, I didn't think the river posed any sort of threat to Halbi's imposing build.

Chief Baha nodded. "We will prepare a raft and canoes while we wait."

I looked to the forests we'd left behind, wondering when the rest of the group would join us. Some had grown faint-hearted over leaving and had lingered behind.

My father voiced his thoughts to Chief. "The others?"

For the first time, Chief's shoulders hunched as he looked around at our people already in the camp, watching them. "The rest will come. Even if we had not given our word, the white man will not let them stay. They will force them to leave."

Since the signing of the Treaty of Dancing Rabbit Creek, which ceded the last of the Chahta land in Mississippi to the United States, droves of our people had left the homeland. The main part of the Removal, overseen by the U.S. government, took three years and hundreds dead to accomplish. Our Chahta Nation of twenty thousand was broken and taken away, forced on a march none wanted to make.

But our chiefs had given their word, had promised we would remove without violence. Some tried to stay, those who wanted to take advantage of the provision in the treaty to remain in the homeland if they became U.S. citizens. But they were attacked and driven out. Just as we would be.

We asked our white neighbors—who had moved into our Nation, who had been friendly—to defend us to their government. These people, who I heard my father speak to in broken English, the way I learned their language, said they were sorry for what was happening to us, but did not want to meddle in the affair.

The time had come for our band to leave.

Not wanting to hear the sadness in the chief's voice, I hurried back to the camp, putting my youthful energy into helping erect a shelter for my mother. It didn't take long, since my friend Ishtaya joined me and soon we were left with little to do. But a jovial voice called to us.

"Time's wasting. You loafers come help me with this canoe."

We bounded to the side of Tushpatubbee, the man who would serve as a scout and camp builder for the long journey ahead. Tushpatubbee, axe in hand, stood beside a tree he had just felled. He was a man of the woods, with no family depending on him.

I admired everything about him, from his coonskin cap and hunting coat with colorful yarn woven in, to his beaded shot pouch and buckskin britches with fringe. He wasn't a giant man—my father was taller—but he had a presence about him that made up for his average stature. He wore his hair long like most Chahta men, flowing loose down his back. On his dark face was always a grin, seeming to widen his narrow jawline.

Over the next several hours, Tushpatubbee had us working on the canoe, while dozens of the other men worked on three more. Soon, he turned the work of this one over to us saying, "You're man enough."

This adage was spoiled when an enthusiastic Chilita, the wise daughter of Halbi, joined us. While her father erected their shelter, she chose to help with the boat preparation.

Though our age, Chilita had the advantage of being a good two inches taller than either of us. She had the soul of an elder but the face of a little girl. I might have thought she was pretty, if I thought of such things, but she wouldn't have appreciated it. Chilita was sensible and straightforward like her father with a square chin to match his, but her round nose and smiling eyes softened her appearance. She wasn't shy nor was she giddy, so I generally didn't mind her being around.

And she was a good friend, so I hid my frown at the intrusion on our manly work with the canoe. Chilita went right to work. Ishtaya smiled and Tushpatubbee chuckled.

Night came.

More of the group straggled in throughout the next day. They bemoaned their losses as evening fell. Whispers of returning to our homes were circulating when a runner stumbled into the light of the cooking fires.

The young man bent over double in front of Chief Baha, gasping for breath. "Fires. Fire, they are burning our homes. Families…escape." He coughed. "Not all."

A wail sounded, and a warrior stomped his foot repeatedly. "Vengeance!" He drew his hunting knife and cut the air. Others joined him, the roars escalating throughout the camp.

"Vengeance, vengeance, vengeance!"

Chief's shoulders slumped. Tushpatubbee removed his coonskin cap and bowed his head, as if helpless to comfort someone mourning the passing of a life. Halbi, the second chief, raised his knife with the others.

Ishtaya stepped next to me. Chilita stood on my other side. We were all afraid.

Chilita stared at her father, then gripped my arm, her fear adding to mine. She whispered to us, "They will be killed. Someone must do something."

Someone did. Someone stepped into the light of the cooking fires, commanding attention. He raised his arms, and suddenly, I remembered a time last harvest. It was after my father had gone to a meeting. A missionary meeting. But he had never spoken of it. Just raised his arms as though imitating someone.

Now he spoke. All listened.

"My kin and blood brothers, I know how you feel about what has happened to you, to us as a people. I too have felt the same and looked for comfort from this wretchedness into which we have been brought."

My father's voice boomed. "The Great Spirit gave us a good land and it pleased our fathers to live in it for many years in peace. They loved their homes and so did we, their children. We lived strictly according to the customs and traditions of our ancestors. They prospered and we thought to have enjoyed the same happy lives, but no, there has come a change and we are in much distress."

I stared as my father dropped his arms, but kept the strength in his words, shoulders straight, head high.

"Why are we surrounded by foes and cast out of our homes? I have thought much about it and I can see only one thing wrong. We must not have pleased the Great Spirit, and if we did not, in what way did we not please him? It must be in only one way, and in a way that is new to us.

"Some time back beyond our old homes I heard a man preach from a book he called *Holisso Holittopa*, a Bible." Pausing, my father opened the pouch that hung around his neck and drew out a small book. He swept it upward, slicing through the air.

"Although this book was read by a white man, I believe there is something better in it than the way the white man acts."

Some murmured in agreement and others grumbled in discontent, but the group of one hundred Chahtas continued listening. My father was a man who commanded respect, but I had never heard him speak on such matters in front of all our people.

He continued. "This book sets the heart right. I know. It makes a new man if he be red, white, or black."

Though there were no black slaves among us, I had seen them in visits to the more wealthy Chahta communities. My father had taught me that all were one people. The blacks. Even the whites. All with one Creator.

My father still held the book aloft. "Let us all take this word and change our hearts so that we forget this great wrong that has been done to us and be better men so that we do not want to kill somebody but want to help them, and we may be better men than we have in this country.

"Maybe we need to do a good to somebody in that new country, and we cannot do this if we go with a butcher knife in one hand and a musket in the other hand like we used to do. We must change our way and live for love of somebody from our hearts."

Lifting his hands again as if the missionary, my father clutched the book and called out, "Those who want to change, to do better, lift your hands without weapons. Stand. Stand now!"

My father spoke with such power, as if he shared a great revelation. Others sensed this too. Knives slid back into their pouches. Almost the entire assembly, including Chief Baha and Tushpatubbee, stood with raised hands.

Chilita released the hold she had on my arm and raised her hand. I raised mine. Ishtaya lifted both hands high.

My father shouted to the darkened sky: "The Great Spirit of our Forefathers, who we now know is *Chihowa*, look down in pity on us today. We have been a hard, cruel, revengeful race of men. We thought this was right. But today we want to do different. Help us to forget these hard ways and live better lives. We are in much trouble now, but don't want to kill or destroy, so give us hearts that we hear about in this book and let us be good, and if we live to see this new country to which we travel, help some of us to do good to those we meet. Perhaps we will not bring shame upon the land."

My father dropped his arms and closed his eyes, as if his words, this speech had taken a toll. Many in the crowd began to talk quietly but they left him alone out of respect.

I looked up to meet his eyes as my father approached. He offered the book and leather pouch to me. "Protect it as you do our seed corn. We must have both to survive."

I swallowed the last of my fear and nodded, taking the book carefully, almost as surprised by this as I had been by my father's speech. He said nothing more as he joined Chief, who was speaking with Tushpatubbee and the headmen.

Chief Baha said, "We have nothing to return to. We cannot move forward until the river's wrath lessens. But this time cannot be wasted. We must move with haste until we reach our new land."

Tushpatubbee drew his long hunting knife from its pouch and a plug of homemade tobacco from a pocket inside his jacket. He sliced off pieces and offered them around. "I already got canoes in the making. How many will you need?"

Chief used his hands to illustrate as he answered. "Four large enough for four men each. They will pull a raft across the river with the supplies and as many of us as it will carry. Many trips will need to be made. It will take days."

Tushpatubbee spat a stream of brown juice to the ground. "You need a raft too, then?"

"Yes. One strong enough not to break apart in the current. We do not want the crossing to be a greater danger than what we are leaving behind."

As if spurred by the urgency of the chief's words, Ishtaya turned back to work on the canoe, but I stood still a moment. I fingered the pages of the book, examining them in the light of the cooking fire some distance away. Chilita leaned over my arm. "What part are you reading?"

I shrugged. "I cannot read it. My mother went to the mission school but it was so long ago, she only remembers enough to teach me a little. Someday I will learn, though."

"I went to the mission school. I have read parts of this book." Chilita touched the pages as though they were sacred. I wondered if they were, so I carefully tucked the book into my father's leather pouch.

Chilita probably knew more of the book than any of us. Though Halbi, Chilita's father, did not like the ways of the white man, he knew education was critical to the survival of our people. But not all the Chahta children had been able to go to the schools taught by the white missionaries.

As the three of us worked, Ishtaya broke the silence by voicing the question we all had. "What should we do about what Kanchi said? How do we please the Great Spirit, Chihowa?"

Chilita brushed back strands that had escaped her folded hair. "We do good. Not only for each other, but for our enemies. We love everyone."

I frowned, sudden bitterness rising up as I bent over and continued hollowing the canoe with my iron adze. I punctuated my words with each whack. "How can you love someone who burns your home? Are there any whites who are good enough to do that?"

Instead of answering, Chilita looked at Ishtaya. "Do you love our people, Ishtaya?"

He nodded, not looking at her. He furiously hacked away at the inside of the canoe.

Chilita poked my shoulder. "All people love their own. There is nothing pleasing in that. But when you love someone not your own, or who has harmed you, how can that not be pleasing to Chihowa? Is that not what your father said is in this book? Did he not say it speaks of better things than what the white man does?"

The pouch lay near my foot. I nudged it with my bare toe. "It is hard to do."

Chilita lifted the pouch and held it in front of us. "But this book tells us how. We must study it. We must know."

I shrugged. "Perhaps we will someday. If the white men do not attack us first."

More quietly, Ishtaya added, "And if we survive the crossing of the great river."

Chapter Two

Days passed, then weeks. Canoes were built, log raft constructed, but still the river's wrath had not completely calmed. The water levels receded, showing a rough path across, strewn with swirling tree branches and sunken logs. Then the announcement spread through camp like the morning light: tomorrow, we would cross the river.

I worked alongside the men that evening as they made final preparations for the crossing. As Chief Baha had arranged, four canoes with sixteen men would tow the raft load by load, until all of our clothing, household goods, provisions and people had made it safely to the other side.

My father tied down the seed corn on the raft, as it would make the first voyage in the morning. I held the load from shifting while my father tightened the ropes.

When we finished, he nodded to me. "Remember, protect the book as we protect the seed corn. Without them, we cannot begin a pleasing life to the Great Spirit when we reach the new land."

I touched the leather pouch that had hung around my neck since the night my father had calmed, then revived the spirits of our people. "I will. Then you will teach us more, won't you?"

My father smiled, a rare sight. "Chihowa will teach us all in His own way. His Son…" He paused, struggling to find the right words. Then he shrugged. "You will understand."

I nodded in respect, turning to help Tushpatubbee carry one of the canoes close to the water's edge for the big day to come.

That night around the cooking fires after the meal, I looked for my friends, Ishtaya and Chilita. I found them seated in one of the canoes near the river's edge. They were listening to my father.

Chilita waved me over without interrupting him. I settled in the bottom of the canoe, pulling my bare feet under me.

My father was imitating the missionary again, face serious as though our souls depended on his words. "The book, Holisso Holittopa, has the words of Chihowa Himself. You must do as it says. Be a good people. Do not drink the white man's whiskey. Do not harm one another. Do not gamble on the ball games and bring yourself to ruin. Do good even to strangers. Be kind to your enemy."

He went on with his admonishments. He'd been doing this every evening. Many of our people had begun to see him as a spiritual leader.

When my father paused, Chilita leaned forward and asked, "Will you tell the big fish story again?"

I settled comfortably back in the canoe as my father began. He was an animated storyteller. The story was one he'd heard from the missionary, but I had a feeling my father added his own words as well. We even laughed at one point. I was certain a missionary sent by the great Chihowa never laughed.

Joy mingled with sorrow, despair with hope, excitement

with fear as the small band of Chahta hurried the next morning and the river crossing was under way. The young children laughed and played and sang about the grand adventure ahead. The old people rubbed against trees to say goodbye. They cried over the departure from our homeland and wondered if they would survive to see the new.

I felt in between the young and the old. I stood with Ishtaya and Chilita, three friends in quiet thought as we waited at the foamy edge of the river.

Tushpatubbee launched the first canoe with his paddle mates, and the men in the other three canoes followed suit. When they were in the water and ready, eight men shoved the raft into the current.

The three women and five children onboard gasped as the river took command of their craft. Chief Baha stood guard on the back of the raft, his voice soothing. The raft rocked, then jerked as the ropes from the canoes tightened and forced it to follow. Finally, the river accepted the fact that the raft was crossing to the other side.

I breathed and Chilita sighed in relief. Ishtaya said, "So many trips to make."

When the first party reached the midpoint of the mile-wide river, the canoes landed on what Chief called Bihi Island. The men hauled on the ropes until the raft was securely clear of the swift current. I couldn't tell what they were doing, but the chief had said the island was the place where they would land if any cargo needed adjusting before making the second half of the trip.

Those on the bank near me crowded closer to the edge, some squinting and whispering. One old woman wiped her eyes in an effort to see more clearly. Then a figure near the canoes waved. I could see it was Tushpatubbee, and I knew everything was all right.

My father assured those who watched by saying, "We are strong. We have good leaders. We will make it through this journey with the help of the Great Spirit. We will become a better people."

The group murmured their agreement.

The canoes launched again and towed the raft behind them. It didn't take as long for the party to reach the far bank as it had the island. The first half of the crossing was more treacherous than the second.

On the far side, the men unloaded the people and belongings from the raft, taking a great deal of time from where I stood. They finally launched once again for the near bank.

I shifted my feet and worried over how long it would take before all crossed. We had started early, and Chief was optimistic about getting everyone across within a week, but I still worried.

The fourth load had been taken across and the raft was being towed back when I felt a hand on my shoulder. I sat in the grass away from the remaining group, content with watching the proceedings since my help wasn't needed. Now I looked up at my father, who had already taken more than one turn in paddling the canoes.

His face looked tired, but his eyes shone. He wore his deerskin jacket with its finely woven diamond pattern wrapping around to the back. "You will cross on this trip with your mother."

I jumped to my feet, suddenly excited to finally cross the river after watching the other trips.

But my father kept a hand on my shoulder. "The river is not under our control. We are at its mercy. But we are more at the mercy of Chihowa no matter what we face in this journey. Remember this."

Anxious to get the last of my things, I nodded and hurried off. I was glad to see Ishtaya and Chilita gathering with their mothers as the canoes landed. We would cross together.

It took longer than I wanted for the raft to be loaded. But with each trip, the men took great care in arranging things so the women and children and old could ride comfortably on the churning water.

At last, it was time to board. I helped my mother climb on before scrambling near the front of the raft where I could see the canoes. Tushpatubbee, Halbi, and Chief Baha were among those who would help tow on this trip. Glancing around, I saw my father take his position as guard on the back, and Chilita and Ishtaya climbed around the sacks of clothing and blankets to join me. A mother with two small children huddled near my father.

A whoop came from Tushpatubbee and the raft jerked out into the current. Chilita gasped and Ishtaya slid a little closer to her. I lifted up on my knees to spot Bihi Island. Suddenly, it seemed farther away than it had from the bank.

The river grumbled and complained beneath us, but didn't toss us about. The rhythm glided up through my body, the gentle rocking of the raft strange comfort in midst of the disaster and adventure we found ourselves in.

Bihi Island swayed in the distance that was closing with each powerful stroke of the sixteen men in the four canoes. I relaxed on my heels. We would soon be across and on our way at last to the new home…

"Ah!"

The raft pitched sharply. I scrambled for a handhold, looking for my mother. I spotted the cause of the shift. A tree, mostly submerged, had slammed into one corner of the raft, sinking it.

Unable to grab onto anything, I tumbled into the frigid river. My head surfaced, a cry I didn't recognize coming from my lips. I shook water from my eyes and tried to swim, but where? How? Each handful of water I reached for entangled me with the blankets as the river took command of my body. I was at its mercy.

No. You are at the mercy of the Great Spirit. He is with you.

Memories of my father's words mixed with screams in the water around me. I caught sight of my father balancing the raft while pulling my mother and the other three women aboard. How could he do it all at once?

Then he looked around, and I knew my father's searching gaze. But I was too far in front of the raft for him to see. I tried to call out, but water replaced my words.

The little children cried out, struggling near the back of the raft. My father dove in and scooped one in his arm while the other latched onto his jacket. He used his powerful arm to paddle close to the raft. The mothers grabbed the children.

With a soggy blanket tangled around my arms and body overcome with shivers, I suddenly lost the strength to stay above water. I gripped the leather pouch still around my neck as I went under.

A rough hand grabbed the back of my neck. I was dragged up and over the uneven edge of a canoe and landed in the bottom. Someone briskly rubbed my chest. I took a breath and opened my eyes to stare at Tushpatubbee.

I coughed, vaguely aware of my mother's scream. I tried to answer. *I'm alive, I'm alive,* I wanted to say but no words came out.

Tushpatubbee wasn't looking at me. His eyes scanned the waters as I lay in the bottom of the canoe. The men above me looked like giants. Their gazes were fierce as they started paddling again. But it seemed we were going in a circle and not even pulling the raft.

Tushpatubbee threw his paddle down by my head and dove into the water.

Chilita? Ishtaya?

With a shout, I sat up and tried to locate my friends. I was so dizzy I couldn't see the raft clearly at first. Then I spotted them. Chilita, Ishtaya, the mothers, the two children. All safely aboard the balanced raft.

Then why were Tushpatubbee, Halbi, and another man in the river, searching the angry waters? Surely, they could pull the blankets in without...

My heart stilled, breath stuck to my cold lips. My father!

My mother wailed and fell forward onto her face. Ishtaya looked at me, then away.

Chapter Three

The gentle rocking was no longer a comfort. It was a mockery. It whispered that even when something seemed peaceful, evil could lurk beneath the stillness.

Tushpatubbee had regained his place in the canoe, silently paddling with his back to me, his shoulders hunched. I didn't move, didn't speak as the little band struggled on to Bihi Island.

I sat in the canoe, legs crossed, hands on my knees, staring at the waters, waiting. Waiting for my father to surface, for the defeated words of Chief Baha to not be true. *He was tangled in the brush and trees in the undertow. We have done all we can to find him. He is no longer with us.*

The canoe dragged through the muddy bottom that surrounded the island as it made a forceful slide onto the bank. The four men piled out and dragged the canoe onto shore, then turned and hauled the shaking raft in. I stayed seated in the canoe, watching.

The men helped everyone off the raft, checking for injuries and offering what little comfort they could. My mother no longer cried. She simply held herself and stared over the river passage we'd just made. Watching. Waiting.

Chilita held her mother's hand. Ishtaya slipped away from them and came to me. He knelt by the canoe, bringing us eye level, but he didn't look at me. Just put a hand on the rim and stared over the waters. Somehow, they seemed calmer now.

Chief's shoulders slumped. "I should not have let him cross so many times. It weakened him."

A wail sounded from the mother of the small children. She gripped the dripping wet young ones in her arms and cried. "Why go on?" she moaned. "Why go on?"

Tushpatubbee hung his head, scrubbed his hands over his face. "I couldn't find him. Tried. Tried hard." He looked to the river. "Don't know what we can do now."

I gripped my knees harder, then let go. My father had given me a charge before the crossing. Now was the time.

Both hands on the pouch that had survived the plunge into the river, I stood and stepped out of the canoe. I carefully withdrew the dampened book and held it up as my father had. But when I spoke, my voice sounded small. "We must go on and honor my father and the truth he brought us. The Great Spirit has given us a guide. He will be with us now, though my father cannot."

I swallowed as faces turned toward me; they were filled with despair, fear, fatigue. "Remember the prayer he made for us, that we may become a better people. We can only do that with the help of Chihowa. And His Son."

With the last word spoken aloud, I understood. I couldn't explain, but I knew. Someday, I would tell them all.

I brought the book down to my chest and bowed my head, unsure what else to say.

But Ishtaya rose and said, "Ome."

Chilita released her mother's hand and came to us, tears in her eyes. "We will study this book. We will help our people."

Tushpatubbee stepped closer and asked, "Will you pray for us like your father did?"

Stunned, I clenched the book tighter. I looked back to the waters, but I knew. My father was gone. I stood in his place now, an unexpected place of great responsibility. For some reason that I think even my father did not understand, Chihowa had given him a revelation to share with our people. Now, for reasons I certainly did not understand, Chihowa had passed that burden on to me and would give me strength to carry it.

Lifting the book high, I prayed, "Chihowa, hear our cries. We are a lost people, a people without hope outside of You. Make us better. Help us understand this book You gave us. Help us get to our new land. Help us to do good there so that the ones who will live on many years from now may prosper and hope in You."

I lowered my arms, still holding the book in front of me. I glanced to each side to include my two friends. We could not comprehend it, but we youths had been deeply affected by my father's words. "Those who want to study this book with us, step forward."

Tushpatubbee put a hand on my shoulder and squeezed. Chief moved closer to us, as did the mother with two young ones in tow. "He sacrificed his life to save my children," she said, arms wrapped around them, hands on their chests.

Most of the canoe paddlers stepped forward. Others, including Chilita's father, Halbi, pretended to busy themselves with adjusting the raft for the remaining journey. Chilita's mother shifted her feet and looked between her daughter and husband.

Ishtaya's mother stepped forward. "He showed how the Great Spirit wants us to love. We must become worthy of that."

My mother walked up to me and put a strangely warm hand on my cheek. She said nothing with her lips, only her soft eyes. Then she dropped her hand and looked at the river one last time before turning away.

I would never forget what had happened that day, never forget my father's death or the transfer of responsibility for our people. I felt the love of Chihowa in my heart. But we still had a long way to go.

After a week of hard work, the crossing was complete with no further tragedies. The party decided to rest a few days before continuing the westward journey, and made a temporary camp on the high ground away from the riverbank. It had been weeks since we'd left our homes, and the fatigue led to sickness among the group. But I still made my request of Chief. The next day, the entire assembly gathered on the riverbanks for a special yaya.

This time, it was me in the inner circle, next to my mother who had covered her head with a cloth. Ishtaya and Chilita, along with their mothers, gathered near, being our most intimate friends. Tushpatubbee stood behind me. All heads were draped with cloths and each person began muttering some expression of sorrow or extolled the good qualities of Kanchi, though his name was not spoken.

The sun was at high noon when we began, but the ceremony went on, with occasional breaks to eat. Finally, the group grew quiet, but no one left. I understood. They were waiting for me to give the final words at my father's grave, words of great meaning and encouragement. I lifted my eyes to the river waters as the sun cast its final glow upon them. I said the words that seemed right, without fear.

"Chi hullo li. I love you."

Ishtaya said, "Ome."

Night came.

Before dawn the next morning, I crept to the river's edge, the book tucked under my arm. It had dried, only a few pages lost.

I sat on a boulder and stared over the waters, grief filling me as tears I'd held back, came. My father was gone. My heart tore and I wept.

But how could I cry in front of the others? Since that

night my father spoke, the people had allowed him to share the Word of Chihowa with them. Now I needed to do what he had done. Would they let me?

I did not know much about the book. But neither had my father, yet he shared what he could. Maybe that was all I needed to do. Share what I'd been given.

So much darkness and evil had already befallen us. But as the first rays of the sunrise spilled over the river, it reminded me there was much light ahead. It was time.

Lifting the book once again, I said, "Ome."

Morning came.

Chapter Four

A cry sounded from a lean-to near the river's edge. I knew what the sound meant. An old woman was dying. She'd gone out of her mind with fever and fear. The old woman's closest relative had abandoned her, panicked over what evil spirits had taken her soul.

Chilita approached the lean-to. It was barely visible from where I stood near my mother's shelter on the high ground away from the riverbank. I seldom left my mother's side, but I did now, the leather pouch pounding my chest at the brisk pace I set to overtake Chilita. I called to her, but she didn't stop. She looked back at me but continued through the high grass and moist ground of the bank.

Chilita motioned me to her. "She needs us. She needs that." Chilita pointed to the leather pouch as echoes of another moan ripped through me. It was time, the first real time to share what I'd been given.

But I wasn't ready. I stopped. Chilita drew back the blanket covering the opening and went inside.

I turned away, covering my ears against the insensible cries. Who could help someone in that condition?

Head down, I bumped into Tushpatubbee, who steadied

me with a log-like arm on my shoulder. "No good."

I looked up at him. He said, "No good to be looking down. Got to keep our heads up and on the sunset every day, Tushpa." He nicked the underside of my chin with his rough finger. "Up."

I looked toward the West, toward the marshy land before us that Chief said we must cross soon. "But what if we can't see the sun at all?"

Tushpatubbee laughed good-naturedly. "It'll still be there."

The old woman died. Three small children soon joined her. We had more funeral cries.

At last, six weeks after leaving our homes too far behind, we were on the move. Chief Baha had ordered ten miles be covered each day, and everyone prepared themselves accordingly.

Tushpatubbee still insisted we could not keep our heads down, and often broke out in a loud song. Children joined in his joyful spirit, causing the woods around us to ring with merriment. But not all could keep the glee or pace.

I watched our band string out as we entered the swamp lands. At best, the ground was waterlogged and soft; knee high muck and stink at worst.

My mother walked before me. I followed in her footprints, easy to see in the mud. A large sack of seed corn was strapped to my back, the leather pouch still around my neck in front.

Protect them, my father's voice whispered to me on the breeze. *I will*, I whispered back without a sound.

Share His words.

I will.

You didn't.

I will.

You must.

I will.

Tired of the commands, I raised my head and saw my fear was true—I could not see the sun. Webbings of moss and vines were layered in the trees we marched through, blocking out light. It was like night had already fallen though it was still morning.

"Move to this side," my mother said, stepping to the right of a small puddle.

Already my bare feet were caked with mud and slime. What harm could dirty water do?

Head down, I sloshed into the puddle and yelped when my body plummeted into the waist-high water.

I tried not to panic, tried not to look as foolish as I felt, tried to shift the sack of corn to where it would be safe and dry as I scrambled in the puddle that suddenly spread out in front of me. I pulled aside the web before my face and stared at the expanse of water stretched out all around, leaving little mud to see.

I heard my mother's soft sigh. I looked to the right to see her hand stretched out toward me. I took it and scrambled back onto the marshy ground that seemed much firmer now. There was a slight path, quite slight, that most of the group followed. The way my mother had directed me. I once again followed in her footsteps. Though gradually, her prints faded in the water.

We sloshed along, heads up, heads down, but always forward, forward. The pace had to be kept. It was a long way to our new home and time had already proved an enemy. The longer the journey, the more would die.

Whether we made the ten miles that first day or not, no one had the strength to care. We made camp for the night in the middle of the swampland. At least, such a camp as we could.

Everyone was in wet clothes, and no fire could be built with damp wood. I joined the other boys and men in gathering as much brush and vines as possible to build up bedding in the watery marshland.

As the group straggled in and huddled together, I noticed that coughing and wheezing had replaced any sounds of the singing we had heard when we started out that morning. Not even a hum circulated to raise our spirits.

I sat cross-legged on the brush near my mother. Ishtaya soon appeared, Chilita at his side. They joined me without a word, but their eyes were expectant.

I opened the leather pouch, withdrew the book, thumbed the pages. A shaft of light from the setting sun caught on one. I made out some of the words, remembering my father saying something similar one evening on the river. I handed the book to Chilita, who could read the English words.

"Our Father in Heaven, hallowed be Thy name…" She read the verses and translated them as best she could, but then hesitated at an unfamiliar word. She scooted close to my mother and held the book to her, pointed the word out. My mother squinted in the fading shaft of light. *"Kashoffi,"* was her simple answer. "Forgive."

My heart burned but when I looked up and saw a dozen faces turned toward us, listening, I held still as Chilita read, "Forgive us as we forgive…"

Lying in the dark, shivering and listening to the coughs that would surely take more lives before this swamp ended, I struggled with the words I'd heard from the book my father had given me charge of. *Forgive.*

Forgive who? The white man who had driven us from our homes? Who caused my father's death? Who pushed me, cold and shivering, to sink in this mire of vines and moss?

But my father's brief legacy could not be ignored. His passion, his belief, his faith were now my own. The thought drove deeply through my very being, becoming a part of me. No. It became me. I wasn't sure I liked it.

There was still a long way to go on this trail of tears.

Chapter Five

It was Keyuchi, a youth a few years older than me, who complained the next day. He walked alongside me, his burden of melon seeds slung over his bony shoulders. "It's only begun. The deaths, the sorrows. These little ones, they don't know but to be happy. They think there's a grand time to be had every day, but we know better." He jabbed at me with his elbow. "Don't we?"

I shrugged and said nothing, my movements slow as I dragged my legs through the mire that sucked and pulled me down. Keyuchi rattled on. "When we get free of this swamp, first thing we'll do is set up a ball field. I heard Chief say we would. See that boy over there? He has a knife I want. I will bet him my day's food for it in the game. Bet that I score and he doesn't."

My ears burned with guilt and the pouch over my heart condemned Keyuchi's words, but still I said nothing. My father had disapproved of the gambling that took place at ball games. The missionaries prohibited ball playing because of the gambling and fighting.

Stickball was for sport, although it was often used to settle disagreements between rival clans. But bets made on the outcome of the game could cause an entire village to become impoverished and all suffered. When the missionaries came to our lands, stickball was one of the first things they discouraged among our people, and forbid at the mission schools.

Keyuchi jabbed me again. "You will be on my team. I saw you play at the harvest celebration last year. We can work together and I'll share the knife with you. Agreed?"

My father hadn't known I played at the celebration. I didn't bet anything, but I knew others did. I was having fun and had tried to ignore the feelings of disapproval my father would have had if he'd known. Not to mention the punishment. The fact that my father didn't watch the games had given me a false security. I carried the guilt now.

I shook my head at Keyuchi, using both hands to pull myself forward through the vine curtain before me. I'd lost sight of my mother, but it didn't matter. There was no easy path. No path at all. "No, I won't play. And I won't gamble. My father would not have allowed it."

"Your father is dead."

The bluntness of Keyuchi's words brought me to a halt. He faced me squarely, arms crossed, the strap of the seed bag clenched in one fist. The confident set of his jaw was intimidating, especially since he stood a head taller than me. His shaggy black hair hung over his eyes, making his brow a constant scowl.

I tried to balance myself like he did in the mud but I staggered and almost fell. Keyuchi laughed loud enough for those passing by to hear. "I shouldn't have asked you. You stumble around like a drunk man."

He slogged on, splashing swamp water up to my eyes. I batted the water away and pulled myself along.

He called over his shoulder, "You will see. More will die. You will die. Live while you can."

Our second night in the swamps was worse than the first.

The stagnant air was considerably warmer than the cold of the high grounds near the great river. Though warmth was welcome, this was a clingy heat that allowed no fresh breeze, no relief. It hung still in the air, filling every space whether I sat, lay, walked.

And the mosquitoes! They were the persistent, constant creature sent to torture us in this pit. I swatted at the pesky devils set on driving us out of our minds. Those of us who were still in our minds. Moans like those I had heard from the old woman who was dying now permeated the camp. Coughs and wheezes.

I sat on a brush pile and alternated between shivering in my damp clothes and panting for a drink of fresh water. It was as Keyuchi said. More were dying. We would all die.

Somewhere across the swamp, Tushpatubbee began a song, but no one joined in. His jovial voice gradually faded with the mist.

I jerked my knees up and wrapped my arms around my legs. The book inside the leather pouch pressed against my heart. I laid my head on my knees. I had no strength to gather my friends to read the verses. No will to share the truth as I'd promised.

Tomorrow. Tomorrow I will.

I caught the voices of Chief Baha, Tushpatubbee and Halbi as they walked near. "Tomorrow we will be clear of the swamps if we keep at this pace," Chief was saying. "Dry ground and open country will welcome us then."

"None too soon." This from Tushpatubbee. "The old and the real young can't take this dampness much more. Fevers are spreading like fire."

A harsh sound came from Halbi. "Some will die before morning. There is no tomorrow for many of us. The journey is too long."

"No choice. We have to try." Tushpatubbee's voice was quiet but strong. "You remember what he said back on the river. He prayed for us. He died, but he left us more than words. He gave us hope. Can't lose that this soon."

That was when I vowed to shed no more tears.

Chapter Six

Without ceremony nor in a single moment, the mud and marsh gave way to solid ground beneath my soggy bare feet. The sun prevailed in this place as the vines and webbing fell away and were replaced by a thicket.

Someone started a song. Perhaps it was inspired by the bark of a squirrel or the call of a crow. Whichever, the song was quickly picked up by the youngest children, who found room to skip and dance through the May apple bushes and redbuds that covered the lowlands in beauty, their blossoms bright and happy. Even the old among us, taking a rest on fallen trees and stumps, smiled at the joy around them. The life.

No more deaths had taken place in the swamps although many still dragged along with fever and fatigue. But fresh air and sunshine was what the medicine man, Attachi, said we needed. He proved correct.

I dropped the bag of seed corn and shinnied up an oak tree, halfway up and beyond. I looked down and saw our band spread out, foraging in the forest with gentle smiles and the occasional burst of laughter. The skinny limb my toes wrapped around and the one my fingers curled over were dry.

Fresh and alive. So were my people.

I gave a whoop for joy. It echoed through the treetops and was quickly joined by shouts from those below. I looked across and saw Ishtaya swinging from one hand on a neighboring oak limb.

Then a commanding whoop sounded. I quickly dropped my way down the tree, scooped up the seed corn bag and hurried along with others who answered the call.

The forest gave way to an open meadow and in the center ran Keyuchi and five other boys. They leaped through the air, bare feet and bronze arms flailing.

Tushpatubbee stood nearby with a grin as he waved at me. "We're staying a few days. Chief ordered a ball field laid here. Get ready! We play this day!"

The world rushed around and past me. I stood still and watched as did the older and sick Chahtas. Their spirits seemed to lift as they watched the activity.

In the meadow, men walked off the appropriate distance of three hundred feet long and thirty-six feet wide and marked it. Four men hacked goal poles from small trees and they sunk these two poles, one at each end of the field.

I watched. Keyuchi glanced my way and scoffed. Still I stood.

The players shouted all around me as they found their stickball pieces among the scant supplies we brought. The playing sticks were two feet in length, with a cup made out of one end and covered with dressed buckskin. A stick in each hand allowed the player to scoop, catch or throw the small, tightly woven ball of leather to a teammate or make an attempt to score by throwing the ball and hitting the goal post.

The game was challenging, a game of skill and endurance. The rules, what few there were, were agreed upon before the start. Tackles, holds, and hits were typically allowed and there was rarely a game without serious injury, though not often deaths.

In the homeland of Mississippi, thousands of Indians and even whites attended the ball games. Dancing, singing, drum playing, and of course, gambling.

I reached up to touch the leather pouch and felt a sting.

"Tushpa!" Tushpatubbee called to me, waving me to come to the center of the field.

All the able-bodied men and boys gathered and quickly separated into two teams. I watched Keyuchi talking to the young man with the treasured knife. Others talked, nods given, bets made.

Tushpatubbee called again. I shook my head and turned away. Only then did I realize I had not stood alone. Ishtaya followed quietly behind me.

We went to where the rest of the company made camp preparations. Weary as we all were, the work was hasty. Most wanted to watch or join in the game about to take place in the meadow.

I helped my mother create a shelter large enough for us by bending and tying branches from a blossom-covered redbud. White blooms fluttered to the ground as we worked. We used a blanket to cover the shelter.

Against the background noise of war-like whoops and the turkey gobble challenges, I gathered wood for fires and found fresh water from a spring.

Suddenly overcome with thirst, I dropped to my knees and cupped one hand through the cool water while holding the leather pouch safely away with the other. I gulped several handfuls, letting the cool taste revive me. I thought of those still in a feverish state in the camp. I thought of the good my father said we needed to do in the new land. To leave old ways behind and begin new ones. It needed to start now.

I stood and carried our water back to my mother. Then I gathered all the remaining water gourds and filled them. In a frenzy to help, I put water pots on to boil for Attachi's medicines, made shelters for the old ones, and gathered enough wood for the next two days.

A warm hand on my shoulder slowed my steps as I carried another armload of wood. I looked up into my mother's gentle face. "Rest. It's time to eat." Despite the harsh trail, her russet skin still shone with youthful health. It gave me hope.

Gathered with some of the mothers and Ishtaya and Chilita, we ate and served the ball players who took turns to refresh and eat. The high spirits brought about by the game were contagious but I admonished myself. My father wouldn't have approved of the game because of the gambling.

Washing down the parched corn and venison with a gulp of the spring water, I opened the leather pouch and pulled out the Bible. Chilita and Ishtaya sat at my side. Out of curiosity—or respect for my father—a few of the women gathered closer.

I opened the book and found a marked passage. The words were underlined with ink. Chilita translated:

> *Blessed is the man that walketh not in the counsel of the ungodly,*
> *nor standeth in the way of sinners,*
> *nor sitteth in the seat of the scornful.*
> *But his delight is in the law of the LORD;*
> *and in his law doth he meditate day and night.*

Chilita stumbled over many of the words, but read on with determination.

> *And he shall be like a tree planted by the rivers of water,*
> *that bringeth forth his fruit in his season;*
> *his leaf also shall not wither;*
> *and whatsoever he doeth shall prosper.*

Chilita moistened her dry lips with her tongue and glanced up at the faces staring at her. Ishtaya whispered, "Ome."

I nodded. A dozen others were sitting cross-legged around us, leaning forward and hanging on every word. Chilita and Ishtaya looked at me with expectation.

So I spoke, trying to remember my father's words, trying to be as wise as he. "We must do good in our new land. We must seek to please the Great Spirit as we have not done in our ignorance." I took the book from Chilita and held it high, wanting to know what my father had felt that night. "Now we are not ignorant. We know the truth. We must know more and more of that truth. We must study this book."

The people that were gathered nodded. I noticed one of the ball players lingering after finishing his meal. He sat on the outside of the circle and propped his head up, leaning forward. I recognized him as the young man with the knife Keyuchi had wanted.

A young girl I knew as Nukwia joined us. Her father, Yakni Foi, was one of the headmen, loud and demanding. He had wanted to return to our homes before word came of the fires destroying them. He wanted to slay the whites even though our chiefs had given their word to harm no one. He had refused the words of my father and forbid his family to listen to him. Yakni Foi played stickball now.

Nukwia made herself small in the outer circle, but I knew she heard every word. If she heeded them, she could tell her father someday. He would be a better leader. Our Chahta people would be better.

Suddenly, I understood it wasn't only those who heard now, who obeyed now that mattered. These would go on to spread the good to others, and they others. It had to be so.

An old man waved one hand at me and motioned to the book. "Read more."

I looked down to the book with pages I knew now to be sacred indeed. I brushed through them to another marked passage. I passed it off to Chilita.

The LORD is my shepherd; I shall not want.
He maketh me to lie down in green pastures:
he leadeth me beside the still waters.
He restoreth my soul:
he leadeth me in the paths of righteousness for his name's sake.
Yea, though I walk through the valley of the shadow of death,
I will fear no evil: for thou art with me;
thy rod and thy staff they comfort me.

Thou preparest a table before me in the presence of mine enemies:
thou anointest my head with oil; my cup runneth over.
Surely goodness and mercy shall follow me all the days of my life:
and I will dwell in the house of the LORD for ever.

Chilita paused. She read it again. And again. No one objected. She read it a fourth time before closing the book gently.

I lifted my eyes to the darkening sky. "This is our prayer to You, Chihowa, God of my father."

Laughter and shouts preceded the returning ball players and observers. Nukwia slipped away. The camp came alive with activity as the players told stories and their injuries were cared for. But it was Keyuchi who caught my attention as he stormed through the camp. He marched up and demanded the knife from his opponent.

The young man frowned in realization. "I did not finish the game. We'll play for it another time."

Keyuchi lowered his head as though about to charge. "Haklo, you know that does not matter. You have no injury, and even if you did, that would not be an excuse."

The young man, Haklo, looked to me and Keyuchi followed his gaze to the book in my hands. Keyuchi snorted. "Oh, I forgot. You are studying the great book. Tell us, Tushpa, does the great book tell us to honor our word?"

I dropped my eyes. "Gambling is wrong."

"So Haklo is wrong! But he still should honor his word, shouldn't he?"

I nodded slowly. I wasn't sure if it was in the book or not, but I knew it was the Chahta way. It was a good way, so it must surely be Chihowa's way.

The knife changed hands. I stiffened when Haklo came toward me. He lifted his hand and clasped my shoulder, hard. But his words surprised me. "You are right, Tushpa. Gambling is wrong. I won't do it again. And to honor my word is good. *Yakoke*. Thank you for being an example of good on this miserable journey."

I lifted my head and nodded, strong on the outside, weak inside. "As my father did, so will I." Yet I did not believe my own words.

Chapter Seven

The company of one hundred Chahtas rested and played for two days before Chief Baha gave the order to continue the journey. Refreshed and rejuvenated, we set out once again, the children eager for the next part of the adventure, wondering at what grand thing lay just beyond their sight. Those who had grown sick in the swamps recovered but still traveled slowly.

We tried to ease their way, but the trail we followed through the dense forest was severely overgrown. It was seldom used, it seemed, and every step contained an obstacle: a fallen tree, briar patches or thick vines to bar the way.

I tried to help an elder over and around and in some cases under these treacherous barriers but he still had to rest often. We fell behind the main body as the group strung out along the trail.

It wasn't wide enough for two and those of us assigned to carry supplies found it even more difficult to navigate. I found a way to tie the sack of seed corn across my back with the leather pouch still in front, but both strings rubbed a raw spot on my neck and shoulders.

When the elder, Poakachi, and I caught up with the main

body, we found Chief had called a council of the headmen. Tushpatubbee was speaking. "Sounds like a smart plan." He lit his pipe. "I have experience at road building, clear cutting, and whatever else you want to name."

Chief nodded to Halbi. "You will lead the men. Stay a day's journey ahead of us. We will follow the trail you cut. We must make the ten miles each day. Assign others to be hunters to provide fresh game for us all. This will strengthen us and make our journey more swift."

Halbi nodded and began selecting the strongest men among us, along with the best hunters. Tushpatubbee conversed with him a moment, then approached me with a grin. "How would you like to join the trail cutters? Beats slow walking and sack toting. You'll be first to see country none in our party has ever laid eyes on."

A tingle of excitement shot through me, but I dismissed it. I had other responsibilities. I glanced around for my mother. She was helping Attachi, the medicine man, tend blisters and sores on various travelers. My mother was a strong woman. I needn't worry over her. And anyone could carry the seed corn. But what of studying the Bible with the others who seemed wont to gather around in the evenings for reading?

Tushpatubbee must have understood my hesitation, because he tapped the leather pouch with his stout finger. "The trail cutters could use someone to keep our spirits up along the way."

This was true, and a real need. I could teach the men about the ways of Chihowa, what I knew of them at least. But when I glanced to the group of men Halbi had finished assembling, my heart trembled. They were the strongest, the bravest. Men who had paddled the canoes across the angry waters of the big river. Men who had tried to save my father. Men who had turned away when I challenged those on the island to follow the Word with me.

These were the ones I would join who had the expectation that boys would behave as men. I rejoiced at the chance to prove myself but things had changed. My position. My responsibilities. My aspirations and dreams. I was no longer a boy learning to be a man. I had become one in my father's place, but not in the traditional sense. How could I suddenly find a place of respect among these men?

All these thoughts flashed through my mind, but before I could reason with myself, I nodded my head in response to Tushpatubbee. "I will."

"Good!" He slapped my back and nodded toward my mother. "Tell her where you're going, and find that rascally friend of yours. He's a good man like you."

In that way, in that time, I knew Tushpatubbee had become an uncle to me and would train me to be a man as my father would have. Somehow, some way, I wanted him to know what I did about Chihowa. And His Son. But not now.

I stood tall a moment, lingering in the praise. Then I hurried to do as he said.

Tools gathered and supplies assigned, we set out before dawn the next morning. But if I'd thought traveling with Poakachi was slow, this was torturous. I realized the immensity of the task, clearing a decent trail for the rest of our people to follow. Scraggly trees had to be felled, brush ripped and hacked away, dead logs dragged clear.

But with a crew of twenty-five men, the work moved along at a better pace than I thought possible. Once my assigned area was finished, I could walk a fair distance that was cleared or being cleared by those before me. I would walk on until one of the headmen told me where to work next. Ishtaya followed along with me, and we made a good team as always, being able to work without saying what needed to be done.

Twice we heard the sound of musket fire and smiled at each other, knowing there would be fresh meat when the sun set. Most of the food would go back to the main body, but some reserved for the men who needed it to continue the laborious work.

We cleared ten miles and then some. The main body was to rest a day before beginning to follow our trail and it made me wonder when I would see my mother again. Ten miles a day was so little compared to the massive distance we had to cover. I wasn't sure exactly how far, none of us were, but it was a long, long way according to Chief Baha.

We set up camp near a stream. We had fresh meat that night, thanks to our skilled hunters. They had killed two deer and trapped three squirrels. Some of the men set about skinning the animals and preserving the hides while others volunteered to trek through the darkness to carry meat back to the main party.

I joined the men who sat around the fire. Already, they wove yarns about the past few days, including exaggerated tales about the ball game and a close encounter with a black bear by one of the hunters.

I could contribute a story to the entertainment and cheerfulness of the evening. But when things quieted and gave me opportunity, I sat without a word.

Finally I withdrew the book. Ishtaya looked at me expectantly, but most of the men ignored me. I thumbed the pages but couldn't read the words as Chilita could. Still, I had thought the presence of the holy book would draw their attention.

Perhaps I should tell a story after all. I slapped the book closed. This gained their attention. "There once was a man who ran away from the Great Spirit."

Men turned their heads toward me, eyebrows raised. Tushpatubbee leaned back against a log, pushed his coonskin cap up his forehead and grinned. Halbi and Yakni Foi stood and walked off into the night.

I cleared my throat, tried to think, tried to remember the story my father told the night before the river crossing. "This man, a prophet, was honored in his village and told of events before they happened. The Great Spirit gave him this gift and gave him the words to say.

"One day, the Great Spirit wanted him to go to the village of an enemy tribe and warn them He was angry with them and would soon destroy them. But the prophet refused to go. He was afraid the Great Spirit would show mercy on the enemy when the prophet wanted to see them destroyed. So he ran away from the Great Spirit. He got into a boat with other men on a body of water larger than anyone in his tribe had ever seen."

I spread my arms wide and gestured with my hands over my head. "Larger than the great river or any great lake. The boat was great, too. But not too great for the Great Spirit. He was angry at the prophet for running away, so He sent a storm to destroy the boat and kill all in it."

The men leaned in to hear better.

"The men in the boat were afraid and asked the prophet why the Great Spirit was trying to destroy them. He didn't lie, but told them it was because he'd run away and that if they threw him off the boat, the waters would calm and they would be saved."

The fire popped loudly and someone jumped. A chuckle went around the group as some of the tension drained. Tushpatubbee shaved tobacco off his plug, stuffed his pipe and lit it without taking his eyes off me.

"But the men were merciful and refused to throw him overboard. They tried to get back to the shore, but the boat began to sink." Here I halted as my throat suddenly constricted.

The boat began to sink…just as our raft had and the river claimed my father.

The parallel was frightening. Had Chihowa been angry with my father, a new prophet to our people?

I jumped up and left the fire, left the objections of not finishing the story. I plunged into the woods we'd fought all day and dropped to my knees. I crawled under the protective limbs of a pine tree, curled into a ball and did not move until morning light.

Chapter Eight

Days passed, then weeks. The trail cutters stayed ahead of the main group, except for the occasions when Chief Baha sent word for a two-day rest and time for all to come together as a family. Sometimes a ball field was set up. We spent extra time finding fresh game. I alternated between staying with the main group and going out with the trail cutters as did others, including women. The elders continued having a hard time of it, but kept pace with the cleared trail.

My mother read to me at times. When I was with our small group of listeners, Chilita would read aloud by firelight and we all talked of the good things we would do in the new land. This group was always receptive. I could count on that. But I never attempted to finish the story I'd begun with the trail cutters, even when prodded by the men.

Had Chihowa taken the life of my father? This I could not understand. My father had not run from what Chihowa called him to do. Unprepared as he was, he willingly stepped into the sight of our people and told them the truth. Told them to put away their weapons, their violent ways. In this, he had averted a war with the whites.

Wasn't that worth Chihowa letting him live? And what of me? Would I be drowned for carrying the words of Chihowa? What if neither I nor my father had been called? I surely never wanted such a position. What was the truth? What did Chihowa want?

From that time on, I dreaded the next water crossing and prayed we would not face one. If we did, I wondered if Chihowa would show the mercy He had not shown my father.

I soon found out.

The trail cutters departed early. Only now we were in marshy lands again, often having to wade through swamps as we tried to mark the best way through for the main group. And then it happened.

Over a small ridge, I joined the men who stood looking over a bayou. It stretched over two hundred feet across with no visible way around except through deep swamp lands or the adjoining lake.

Tushpatubbee nodded at Halbi. "You're right. Rafts are the best way across. We should be able to pole all the way. It'll take a few days to get everyone across. The water's plenty calm though."

Plenty calm. This did not describe the churning in my belly. No matter that this wasn't the mighty river with its terrible current and hidden trees that could sink a raft. All that mattered was that we had to cross on rafts. In deep water. Water deep enough to drown a young prophet who refused to share Chihowa's Word to those he was called to.

I trembled and reminded myself of my vow not to cry no matter how frightened or guilty or sad I felt. But I could not control this fear.

As the men spread out in the dense woods around us and began the process of building rafts, I ran away and shinnied up one of the old cypress trees near the water's edge. I hid myself among the branches and pulled out the Bible. I thumbed the pages, looking for highlighted passages, wishing I could read and understand all of what the whole book meant. Or at least something that would ensure me I wasn't about to die.

Panting with anxiety, I thumbed to the back of the book. All the way to the end, but understood nothing, nothing to strike me with conviction that no doubt could overcome. I needed to know my father hadn't died in vain. I needed to know I wouldn't die.

I closed my eyes. Words came to me, softly spoken by my mother's tongue with tears in her voice. I spoke the words to myself, making sure my ears heard as my soul felt.

"Greater love has no man but that he give his life for his friends."

I broke my vow to not shed another tear.

Our people made the crossing over three days and without incident. I took more than one turn on a pole, sinking it into the mud beneath the water, leaning on it and walking to the back of the raft, pushing the raft forward in harmony with three other men on poles. Over and over. I stared down at the water each time. The reflection showed the leather pouch hanging around my neck. I felt no fear.

The third night, I finished the story.

"There was a man who ran away from the Great Spirit," I began. Those around the main fire turned to me, intrigued. I noticed some of my fellow trail cutters move in closer, knowing the story would be finished at last.

I retold the first part as more gathered, then moved on to the second half. "The boat began to sink and the men could not save it. Finally they threw the prophet overboard and prayed for the Great Spirit to forgive them and not charge them with his life. The water calmed and they lived.

"But the prophet sank down, down to the bottom. He lay in the mud as he prepared to die, but just then…" I paused as my father had when telling the story. I opened my arms wide toward my captive audience. I closed and slowly opened my arms. "A giant catfish—such as no man had ever seen before—sucked the prophet into his mouth and swallowed him!"

Children giggled while the adults gave a mixture of uncertain chuckles and horrified gasps. I rushed the words, intensifying them. "The prophet lay in the belly of that catfish for three days and three nights. But he did not pray to live. He prayed for the Great Spirit to forgive him and that he would always obey Him from then on.

"Well, after three days in the slimy belly, the Great Spirit sent another storm and the catfish washed up to the shore and spit the prophet out on dry land. Once he realized he was still alive, he knew what he must do."

A little boy seated in the crossed legs of his mother waved his arms. "He cut up that catfish and ate *him*!"

A roar of laughter went around the group, drawing even more people to my fire. I chuckled and shook my head. "No. The catfish was used by the Great Spirit. He lived on." I leaned closer to the boy, lowered my voice and winked. "He may be in the next waters we cross."

The boy's eyes widened and he glanced up at his mother. He scrunched down further and grabbed her arms, locking them around his chest.

I continued. "When the prophet dried off, he set out for the enemy village. But they weren't happy to see him. They threw dirt and rocks at him and cursed him. But he took up a drum and beat it while he walked through their camp for three days. He warned them the Great Spirit was angry with them and would destroy them because of their wickedness. And what happened?"

I leaned back as all waited for the answer. "They listened to the prophet. They burned all their weapons. They gave back ponies they had stolen from the prophet's village. They begged the Great Spirit to forgive them. And what happened? He did! He showed them mercy, as He has shown our people mercy."

A loud harrumph sounded from the back of the group. Keyuchi stepped into the light, arms crossed. "Do you mean we are like the wicked enemy tribe? I'd say that is the whites. They are the ones the Great Spirit should destroy, not us!"

The Chahtas murmured agreement with sadness and defeat. I shook my head, trying to find the right words. *Finish the story*, my father whispered to me.

"No. You are wrong, Keyuchi. The Great Spirit destroyed no one and had mercy on the wicked people. But what of the prophet? After all that had happened, of the mercy shown him even, was he happy? No! He was angry with the Great Spirit for saving his enemy. He was bitter and never knew peace again."

Keyuchi turned away, but the murmurings quieted. The people were satisfied to think of the whites like the prophet, bitter and without peace.

But there was more to the story. Chilita voiced it. "If we seek forgiveness and change our ways, Chihowa will show us the mercy that was prayed for us, and we will be a happy and whole people in the new land."

The group sighed in relief and began to stir. Night crawled around us and it was time for sleep. There was still a long way to go.

Chapter Nine

B are feet, scant clothing and the lack of proper nourishment led to more sickness among us in the following weeks. I did what I could—carried the seed corn, joined hunts, gathered wood, worked with the trail cutters to make the way easier on my people. But it was never enough. Fevers broke out again as we traveled through yet another swamp.

My mother's voice called softly to me one evening. "Tushpa." She sounded tired, so tired I felt fear as I plodded through the mud toward the shelter she was in. The mud grabbed my feet and refused to let go without a fight. I was tired of fighting, but there was nothing else to do.

I pulled aside the blanket that tried in vain to keep the damp away from Poakachi. He was the elder I had helped when the long walk began, back before the trail cutters started.

Poakachi was reclined on a brush bed. I knew my mother had likely made it. She was seated by his side, his withered hand in hers. She looked up at me. "We must read to him from the verses. Pray for him. He is dying."

Poakachi's eyes were glazed over when they turned to me, but still managed to stab my soul. His gaze frightened me, put too much expectation on my weak shoulders.

I lifted the leather pouch from around my neck and handed it to my mother. "You read and pray. I must return to my work. We have to find dry wood and game before we all die."

My mother accepted the pouch but her eyes pierced me. "We do not need physical nourishment only."

Whatever else she might have said was unspoken as I left the shelter. The hacking coughs of the dying man followed me. His closest relatives had left him, knowing the feverish state he was in and fearing evil spirits might invade them as well.

I stopped in the midst of the slow activity of camp building by the people who had become as my own blood kin. Such a large family. Why did I feel responsible for them? I was only a boy, the son of a man who had become respected for his spiritual insight.

Chief Baha was responsible for guiding us all safely to the new land. Was I responsible for their souls?

I could only give what I'd been given.

I raised my voice to be heard even by those scattered through the swamp, searching for dry wood. "Greater love has none of us than this, that we give our lives for each other!" A few of the weary heads turned to me, eyes downcast.

I don't know if any believed or would respond to my words, but I had given. I set about the business of saving the lives I could, but Poakachi's eyes haunted me. Why could I not stay with him? Why could I not stay with the old woman? It wasn't evil spirits I feared. It wasn't death. I would have given my life for them. What was it?

Two elders and one child died before we reached the end of the swamp. I was numb to the deaths, feeling little during the funeral cries. We saved all we could; now we had to move on.

Through the woods, across the rivers, down through more swampy lands. How long had it been? Chief Baha kept the record. Nine weeks since leaving our homes. We'd seen little of anything except hardship. None of the other Chahtas who had left the homeland were on this trail. No settlements along the way. Nothing but wilderness and tears.

Ishtaya and I broke away from the main group and went on a two-day hunt. We killed a deer and brought it back to the camp. After butchering it, I turned the meat over to my mother and went about preparing to tan the hide. Perhaps Ishtaya and I could make moccasins in the new land.

But it wasn't to be.

I heard his growl before I realized old Choswa was upon me. Known as a shoemaker, he was ornery and loud-mouthed and had always paid me little mind. He was wrapped in a bearskin hide, his long braids flanked over his shoulders.

Clambering over me where I sat, he grabbed the deer hide I was working on and yanked on it. I frowned and pulled back but froze when he put his snarling face in mine.

"You little weasel, hand it over!"

I scrambled back. Choswa rolled the bulky hide and jerked it under his bearskin before sulking off into the woods. I knew the hide would never be mine.

I was angry. As angry as I had been at Keyuchi's insults. As angry as I had been at being uprooted from my home.

I kicked at the dirt before letting my legs splay out before me, leaning back on my hands. I felt more like a little boy than I had in three summers.

"Old Choswa after you, too, eh?"

I wanted to ignore Tushpatubbee, wish him away, but he sat down next to me, his knife and tobacco plug bundled in one hand while he leaned back on the other, putting us eye to eye. "That old Choswa, he's a menace but a needed one. We'll get him to work soon as we stop long enough to get something lasting done."

"When will that be?" I spit the words through my teeth.

My eyes were on the tips of my mud-caked toes.

"Oh, before you know it. Yes, we'll be coming into civilization and be back among our people soon—"

"You say that," I interrupted. "You say it, Chief says it. No one believes it's true any more than they believe the words we read." I shook my shoulders to make the pouch around my neck sway.

"That what's bothering you, then? That they don't believe the book...or they don't believe *you*?"

I released my grip on the ground and lay flat, staring at the tree branches overhead, trying to make sense of the splashes of sun coming through. "I want to go home. I want my father to be alive. I want this journey to end. That is what I want."

Tushpatubbee gave me a respectful silence, though I didn't deserve it. Finally, he said, "You just keep on. Keep on praying for all of us. We need it."

And that was all the help he offered. But it was enough.

I lay there a long time, alone, thinking on my uncle's words. When had I last prayed for our people? Not in front of everyone, with eyes looking to me. When did I last pray for forgiveness, to forgive others as I had been forgiven? When had I earnestly prayed to Chihowa for my people? I closed my eyes.

Look down on us, Father. Forgive us. We—I forgive those who have wronged me. Teach me Your way. Teach me to teach others. Please.

Chapter Ten

A week later, we came to a great river like the one that began our journey. Chief Baha said it was the Arkansas River, and it would lead us to a post called Little Rock. The name excited me because I knew Arkansas Territory was near the Indian country where we were headed. While the river itself did not excite me, it did not frighten me either. But we didn't know if we should cross now or follow it a ways.

Our company made camp on the bank. The next morning, I set out with Tushpatubbee and headman Yakni Foi to scout a way to the post road we were to travel on to Fort Smith. Chief said he wanted to conserve the energies of the sick and weak in our band. I was honored he chose me to help in the scout.

But I knew my place. I followed along behind Tushpatubbee who was in the lead with Yakni Foi following, and me last on the narrow deer trail that ran along the bank. Yakni Foi paid me little mind. He did not like when I asked someone to read from the white man's book, but he had yet to catch his daughter, Nukwia, lingering around during those times. He seemed a man bent on hate no matter what, and he expected the same of his family.

Tushpatubbee and Yakni Foi conversed about how far ahead the road might be and how easy a time our people would have if they came this way. But a strange sound caught my ear.

I paused, letting the men continue ahead. When I made out the sound clearly, I gave a low whistle that caught the leaders' attention. They turned back and I motioned up the embankment that disappeared from sight. The sound drifted down from there.

Tushpatubbee came back to my side and cocked his head. He nodded to me and found a way to scramble quietly up the embankment, me following behind with Yakni Foi. Still concealed by trees, we hunkered down and observed the sight before us.

A man was seated on a barrel laid over on its side in front of a ragged looking cabin while he dragged a long stick across an odd-looking wooden instrument. It made a pleasant sound. The man wasn't old, wasn't young. He just was, with his long beard and coonskin hat and a yard full of children playing.

I watched the scene as a woman came to the doorway holding an empty cast iron pan, a corncob pipe between her lips. She leaned against the door frame and listened to the sounds as they repeated over and over.

Tushpatubbee glanced at Yakni Foi and me. The head-man frowned with disdain, his fingers tracing over the handle of a hatchet in his belt. But my interest was different and apparent. Tushpatubbee grinned and moved forward from our cover.

"Halito!" he called in our mother tongue then added in broken English, "Hello. We look for the post road to the place called Little Rock." He motioned to the road we could now see that ran alongside the shack. "Where this one go?"

The children scrambled from the yard and into the doorway with the woman and gawked at us. The man never lowered his instrument. "Shucks, it don't go nowhere, son. It's there in the morning time and there in the evening time and always around."

I had trouble making out his crude words in the strange tongue, so I listened intently as Tushpatubbee continued in English, walking into the yard while the children stared and the woman kept smoking her pipe. "You know where river goes?"

"It just stays put right there."

"You own this place?"

"Nope. It owns me."

Yakni Foi crossed his arms with a scowl and looked at me. I knew he spoke little, if any, English. I quietly interpreted to him what I could, while watching the white family watch us.

"You have food to sell?"

"Don't have food to eat."

The sounds played over again, the tune becoming tiresome. My eyes darted around the yard. It wasn't so different from home in some ways, more so in others. I didn't recognize the use for the wood bin a young boy sat on while swinging his bare feet and looking back at me. A young girl stood just inside the doorway near the woman, combing her hair and holding something that reflected her face while she ignored the conversation that was growing more useless word by word.

"You have well?"

"I'm well enough, thank ya."

"Why you not play whole song?"

"I'm partial to the part I know."

With this, Tushpatubbee moved closer and motioned toward the instrument. The man grinned and handed it over. I watched, stunned, as Tushpatubbee held the instrument as the man had and ran the stick across the wood. Now that we were closer, I could make out hair-like string on the stick and strings on the wooden instrument.

Tushpatubbee made the odd contraption sound as the man had, only he played more. And more. The boy on the wooden box clapped his hands along with the sound. The littlest children jumped to their feet and rushed back into the yard as the sounds grew louder and more cheerful, no longer monotonous. The children danced, barefoot and in night-shirts. They grabbed hands and swung each other around until they fell to the ground. The man jumped up and clicked his heels, tossing his coonskin cap into the air with a whoop. The woman and girl laughed.

Tushpatubbee let out his own whoop, bore down on the instrument a final time and ended the tune with a flourish and a twirling of the stick.

He grinned and offered the instrument back to the man who took it with a grin of his own. "Son, you can come on in and find yourself a spot and something to eat. Yes sir, we'll scrap up enough to feed all you Indians. I reckon you've had a long walk and more ahead. Name's Homer and that's my gal, Sally May. We got a keg of whiskey hid away under the bed. Have a swig and tell us a story and I'll take you on to the post road first thing in the morning."

To my surprise, neither of my leaders objected to the man's offer, even after I translated it to Yakni Foi. He merely shrugged and agreed.

I soon found out why.

The next morning, Tushpatubbee and I were ready to set out with the man, Homer. Yakni Foi was not. He could scarcely stand and each time he did, he vomited. At first I feared he was ill as so many in our band were. But when Tushpatubbee just shook his head and forced Yakni Foi to walk, I understood the real reason.

Yakni Foi had drunk much of the whiskey Homer had offered the night before. This was the aftereffect. I under-stood why the missionaries had forbidden whisky among our people and why my father had been so set against it. But many still found it when they wanted. Such as now.

It sorrowed my heart and I vowed not to tell Nukwia what her father had done. Nor would I tell Chief Baha. I did not know what Tushpatubbee would do. I only knew I had not seen him take a single sip of drink, even when offered several times.

We trekked along the trail above the riverbank, following the whistling Arkansas man who hooked his thumbs through his suspenders and seemed to enjoy the flittering martins above us. I liked the birds as well, at home in Mississippi. They ate thousands of mosquitoes. I wished to see them in the swamps we had come through, but surely no more swamps or sickness or death lay ahead of us now. We had to be close to our destination.

Yakni Foi followed several paces behind, so I kept up with Tushpatubbee and Homer as they conversed with animated hands.

"How did you learn to play the fiddle?"

"Spent winter in Virginia, nothing else good to do."

"What a hoot! Imagine an Indian knowing how to fiddle. None of them others gave a hoot about it. Least none I saw. Most of 'em had their heads so down couldn't tell if they had any eyes at all. Shame, shame what's happening to you folks. But I reckon it's good at least to have a place to go that'll always be your own now."

"How many come through? Chahtas?"

Homer raised his bearded chin and scratched it. "Oh hundreds I reckon. No, thousands for sure."

I still marveled at how unclean the whites were. In their cabin, I had hardly wanted to touch anything. The lack of clean water to wash in had been torturous for my band coming through the swamps. We were used to going to the water every morning and washing. Tramping through mud and muck for days at a time had been trying.

But these whites lived by a river! They could wash themselves and their whole cabin easily. The image of the cabin with its haphazard shingles came to mind. Perhaps that was one good thing about not repairing a roof; it let rain water wash the inside of the place. I chuckled to myself.

It must have come through aloud though. Tushpatubbee

looked back at me with a wink and spoke in Chahta. "I see you find these whites as funny as I do. These seem like good folks though. I've been around worse."

Homer looked back at me as well, as he kept tromping forward without looking at the trail. "You sure are a quiet sort. Whatcha got in that bag around your neck? Something to ward off evil spirits?"

I touched the leather pouch, and suddenly felt shy. But I raised my eyes to look at the man. I wondered if I would be the last impression he ever had of Indians. "I carry Bible. It ward off more than evil spirits."

The man hooted and slapped his leg without missing a step. "Well I'll be! An Indian with religion. I'll bet you have the ear of the Almighty more than I ever have."

Silence settled over the group. We listened to Yakni Foi, somewhere behind us, vomiting again. The martins continued their pleasant songs. Nearby, the rush of the river sounded both inviting and threatening.

A morning's walk later we came to a solid, sandy loam road going west and east. Homer waved up the road. "This be it, boys. That there way takes you clean to Little Rock, though they don't cotton much to Indians in town. Just stay north of the river, what's called North Little Rock. That's where the government agency is that'll get you fixed up and going again. At least, I reckon they will. Now, I'll be seeing you folks when you pass by my place again. I'm going to walk on in to Little Rock and see about begging me another keg of whiskey. Your friend drained me dry!"

Waving, Homer set out, whistling the tune and taking a skipping step now and again as he danced up the road.

Yakni Foi caught up to us and crossed his arms, but not before I saw his hands trembling. How could any man let such a vile drink take over his mind and body?

"You are fools to follow the white man!" Yakni Foi spit in the dust near our feet.

Tushpatubbee shook his head as if in pity and turned to me. "What do you say, Tushpa? How about we hunt up a squirrel or two between here and the man's cabin and leave it with his wife? We need to thank them proper for letting us stay, feeding us and showing us the road."

"You should not trust them!" Yakni Foi jabbed a finger toward the road Homer had taken. "He and his friends will lay a trap for us and ambush our whole company. We do not know if this is the right road. He would send us to be lost and die in the wilderness!"

He started to turn away as if expecting us to follow, but Tushpatubbee didn't move. I stayed rooted, looking between the men who now faced each other. I wished Chief were here. Or my father.

The latter thought came unconsciously and it saddened my heart. I was thankful Nukwia still had her father. I only wished hers was a man like mine instead of Yakni Foi.

Tushpatubbee eyed Yakni Foi while handing me his musket. "Keep a sharp look out for squirrels. We may get enough to take back to our camp."

Yakni Foi jerked away and went down the trail we had come up. I wondered why he had come this far. It was doubtful even he could answer that in his condition.

Chapter Eleven

The sun was straight up when we left Homer's cabin after delivering two squirrels to Sally May. She fed us of the fish her boy had caught and fried. A full stomach and conversation almost made me forget the hardships we'd overcome. Almost.

Once we entered the woods on the trail near the river, Tushpatubbee set a swift pace I found hard to match. At times I had to scamper into a run to catch up. The scout never looked back at me, giving me confidence that he felt I could keep up. I did.

We kept this pace until evening when the near-summer sun found a place to sink into the night. I smelled the fires first, then heard the sounds of my people as we neared camp. Tushpatubbee increased his pace again and soon we were in the midst of our people.

Ishtaya and Chilita saw me and rushed forward to welcome us back. I did little to return their greetings as I followed Tushpatubbee to Chief Baha who was in a circle with the headmen. Yakni Foi stood with arms folded. Halbi stood by him, his expression dark.

Chief did not look pleased to see us. "Tushpatubbee, you

will no longer lead in scouting. I am disappointed with the report of you. And you." Chief nodded to include me, making my head light. He continued. "You both are a disappointment to us. You must work to mend the trust we had given. Now go, help with the building of the raft. We begin crossing in two days."

I wanted to slink away, into the woods in pretense of gathering firewood, of being a little boy again.

But I stood with Tushpatubbee, who waited until Chief had nothing more to say before he spoke in his calm voice. "The book Tushpa here carries, it says we are to hear two sides of a story before condemning someone as guilty. You best hear my side or we might end up with more problems, like someone drowning at this fierce point in the river."

These words caught the attention of all who were nearby. Yakni Foi said nothing, his expression blank.

Chief Baha looked at us as if for the first time, though with suspicion still in his eyes. "To say anything other than what we have heard would be to call an honored member of our council and a headman a liar and detriment to us all. Is this what you want?"

Tushpatubbee shook his head. "No. It's not what I want. But I can't let my people be put upon with more hardship when there's an easy road for us to walk straight on to North Little Rock and the government agency that has our supplies."

This caused a stir among those listening and more people moved closer to us. Chilita stood near her father, Halbi, quietly watching with Ishtaya at her side.

Chief looked between Yakni Foi and Tushpatubbee and me, his head turning, always watching. "I will hear your words."

Tushpatubbee recounted the events of our adventure, though he left off the part about the whiskey Yakni Foi drank. He wove the tale so well and compellingly, even I had troubled sorting what was true and what was cleverly devised to make it entertaining and convincing.

When he finished, I felt weight in the air, the sense of

dread as those nearby exchanged looks. I wondered what kind of tale Yakni Foi had woven and wondered which of the men everyone would believe. I prayed it was Tushpatubbee. Yet that would cast Yakni Foi in an irreparable light, condemning him as a troublemaker and an unworthy headman. He deserved such. But perhaps not on the whole. He had done many things to serve our people the past two and a half months.

I could not judge, and simply added, "Chief, we completed the work you sent us to do. We did not all agree on the best way. You must make that decision."

Chief stared at me in surprise. I met his gaze. He nodded and looked around the circle and to all the people who hovered near, waiting to hear the outcome. "We have worked hard to come this far. We are not afraid to work more. But if Tushpatubbee was able to find a safe way to the post—despite whatever means he might have used—we will yield to that as the Great Spirit's blessing on us. We leave in the morning for the road."

I turned away and went to the fire my mother had built. She handed me a bowl of corn mush for my evening meal. Her warm hand touched mine and I looked up to see her smile. My mother did not often smile, especially on this trail, but it was one of encouragement. Still, I had trouble smiling back. I sensed she had something to tell me, something she did not quite approve of.

I didn't want to hear it now, especially if it had to do with the rumors Yakni Foi had spread around camp about Tushpatubbee and me. Surely my own mother did not believe the lies! But then, I had not been as attentive to her in the past week or so, being preoccupied with other work. And I had felt myself growing. I would always heed my mother's wisdom, as women were the life givers of our nation. But I was also becoming a man.

My mother spoke. "The people are happy today because we reached the river. But they will be sad again. They miss home and our old ways and old life. Many will lose heart if we do not encourage them."

"I have." I bit out the words, agitated that she didn't acknowledge all I had done for our people at my young age. Even when I didn't want to. "Do you not see me sharing the book with them and telling them what Chihowa says we are to do?"

"But do you do it in your own heart?"

I spooned the mush into my mouth, taking hot gulps while I tried to calm myself. How had my mother known my thoughts, my struggles? She probably knew how my pride had increased when Chief chose me to help scout a river crossing. How I had ignored my closest friends when they needed me. How I harbored anger and hate in my heart, though I knew it was wrong.

I sighed, setting the empty bowl aside. Eyes still down, I said, "It is not easy."

"No. But you cannot expect others to do what you do not do yourself. Teach them how to forgive by forgiving. You've done well. But you must do it the way Chihowa teaches. As your father did."

Hurt and infuriated with myself, I raised my voice. "I am not my father!" Jumping up, I scrambled out of the shelter.

I charged toward the woods and straight into Yakni Foi. He pushed me back and spit on me. "You will never again humiliate me before our people. You are a boy, not a man, or I would kill you for what you did."

I stepped away from him, knowing he was meaner than ever in his condition. But I also knew he only had the courage to threaten me, a boy as he said. He would never confront Tushpatubbee. "You bring shame to our people with the white man's drink."

I turned and ran toward the west.

Why had the sun already set? I wanted to see it, over the land we would never reach. It was a hopeless effort and I was tired of being part of it.

Chapter Twelve

"You called my father a liar." Nukwia slipped up behind me as I talked with Ishtaya and Chilita. When I turned, pain flickered across Nukwia's face.

The rest of the camp made preparations for sleep. We had not studied the book this night as I had hoped when coming back. There was still too much uncertainty and distrust among the people. I didn't know what to do. Or how to respond to Nukwia's quiet but harsh words now.

So I said nothing as I stared back at her. Her hair was folded up and tied, but strands fell around her dark face after the long day.

Nukwia wrapped her arms around herself. "And I know the truth. He did lie." Her chin dropped. "He was so angry when he returned. He accused you both of drinking with the whites when it was he who had the smell of whiskey on his clothes."

A tear ran down her cheek and it made me angry. Angry that Yakni Foi would add to our sorrows this way. I sputtered, "If he hates the whites so, why does he seek their wild drink? This will be the ruin of our people!"

Ishtaya put a cooling hand on my shoulder. "The temptations in the world are great. What Yakni Foi did was wrong, but we should pray together that he seeks forgiveness from Chihowa and from those he has wronged."

"You pray." I spit the words, but when Chilita raised her eyes to the sky, I gave in and raised mine as well but said nothing. I wasn't sure what Nukwia did.

Ishtaya prayed. "The Great Spirit of our fathers, look down in pity on us. We do not know all Your ways and the ways we do know we do not always follow. Forgive us of these ways. Forgive our brother Yakni Foi. Show him the way to You."

A harsh laugh brought my eyes down and into the eyes of Keyuchi. He scowled at us. "You act righteous as though you are sons of the Great Spirit Himself. But you are not. And you are wrong to befriend whites. Wrong!"

Nukwia darted away in the darkness. Keyuchi moved closer to me, nose almost touching mine. "You will pay for this wrong. You will pay for betraying our people to them."

Homer, Sally May, and their yard full of children paraded along the trail toward the road with us. Homer played the fiddle and the children danced and Sally May passed out corn muffins.

At first, most of my people were shy and uncertain but soon they joined in the merriment. There was no language barrier in laughter.

When the cheerful company reached the road, Homer and his family said their goodbyes.

He pumped Tushpatubbee's hand. "You ever this way again, stop off and fiddle us a tune. Do that one we'll call the Choctaw Traveler. It's a right smart piece, almost as smart as me!"

Tushpatubbee laughed and heartily agreed. He was a traveling man.

That made me think on how, once we reached the new

land, my uncle would move on and I'd never set eyes on him
again. The thought saddened me and preoccupied my mind as
my people gained the road and began the trek to Little Rock. I
once again carried the seed corn.

When we arrived at North Little Rock, I quietly went
about my duties as Chief ordered our camp set high above the
river, putting the mighty Arkansas between us and the main
town of Little Rock. In previous years, Chahta parties had
crossed on the ferry and camped near Little Rock before continuing on south to the Red River country.

But we were headed northwest toward Fort Smith and
would cross the river somewhere up on the Military Road. We
would settle in at North Little Rock for a short time and re-
group, let the sick and weak recover, replenish our supplies,
learn what lay ahead from here.

I stayed close to camp the first day. Chief Baha, Halbi
and Tushpatubbee went to the log cabin that served as the Indian Agency to speak with the agent about food and how to
proceed. I wanted nothing more than to stay among our people and share the teachings from the book and never again
find myself caught between two factions of our leadership.

When things were settled for the camp, Ishtaya and
Chilita urged me to go exploring. We found a trail leading
high above our camp. It was marked with sandstone and slate,
a rough path. At the top of the trail we found a bluff over-
looking the lowlands around the river.

The town of Little Rock lay on the other side of the
mighty river, a settlement of over five hundred people with
dozens of log cabin stores and a few frame houses scattered
about. The main part was situated on a high bluff above the
river with a steep climb from the ferry. A rock jutted out on
one side, a smart looking place to dock a boat or even several.
The river was wide at this point and we had heard rumors that
giant steamboats could turn around here when the water was

high enough.

Chilita pointed to the ferry. "Many of our people crossed here but they weren't taken to town because the whites feared they carried cholera from the Mississippi. It was true. The whites in Mississippi had given them the disease on the steamboats before they came. Many, many died."

In all the walking we had done up to this point, I'd occasionally envied the stories I'd heard of our people who were able to ride the steamboats for weeks instead of walking. I no longer envied them.

There were few structures on this side of the river, in North Little Rock. The buildings included a tavern and stables and a public house for travelers who arrived after dark, too late to ride the ferry. I wondered what the place was like but had little thought of finding out.

Mainly I wondered if there was any food to be had here for our people.

When our leaders returned before nightfall, they shared the news. Although the government man, Captain Jacob Brown, had been civil, he hadn't been as much help as we needed. The crops promised him had not come, nor the money to pay for them from the bank in Louisiana. A massive flood the summer before on the Arkansas had taken out crops and farmland for miles. He was helpless to do much, though he did offer a small supply of corn and dried beef. It would be enough for each of us to have a handful a day on the rest of our journey.

Chief tried to encourage us by saying the Military Road built to help in the Removal was a good one and we could follow it all the way to Fort Smith. No more swamps or rivers to cross or road building.

Most of our people took all this in stride, neither bemoaning nor celebrating but continued with the work to be done while we camped near the post. It was Tushpatubbee who sauntered over to old Choswa, who muttered to himself while he laid out leather from a hide he'd preserved along the trail.

"Well, what do you say, old man? Time to make us some new moccasins and such, you think? What ones have them are worn through and sure would make it an easier time for the others."

Choswa swung an arm at Tushpatubbee, shooing him back. "Talk to your government man. He's to help the poor ignorant Chahta!"

I moved in closer to hear and noted I wasn't the only one. More than a few of us needed shoes or repairs made to ones we had. I had walked the whole way thus far barefoot.

Tushpatubbee pulled out a new plug of tobacco I assumed he obtained at the Indian agent's office and shaved off bits for his pipe. He lit it and smoked while Choswa got on all fours over the hide and grumbled while he inspected it. "Government men. Puh! They drive us out, starved and naked, burn our homes, kill our stock. Puh! They steal our land, say we are savage. Puh! Think we are too dumb to know how to find our own heads. Puh! White man no good. No good to the Chahtas at all. Puh!"

A small circle of impatient people stood around him now, and an elbow nudged me. It was Chilita. She nodded her head to old Choswa but I frowned. What could I say to the man? I didn't like him, especially since he'd taken my deer hide. Probably the one he prodded even now.

But then I realized others in the circle, including Tushpatubbee, looked to me. They expected me to help somehow, as if I could persuade the cantankerous, stubborn old Choswa to make us shoes for the journey just because I was the one who helped them study the book.

If agitation counted for anything, I had plenty of that. Arms crossed and determined, I stepped forward to the edge of the hide and looked down at the man. "We cannot do anything about the government. We are here, we will survive, we will bring honor to the Great Spirit and our ancestors in the new land. Now, will you make us moccasins from the hide that belongs to us all?"

Before I finished speaking the last word, old Choswa

grabbed my ankle and yanked my foot out from under me. I landed hard and howled, teeth clanking together and rattling behind my eyes.

Choswa pulled my foot to him, stuck his thumb at the end of my heel and his forefinger at the tip of my biggest toe. He grunted and shoved my foot away. "Just ask."

So it began. Old Choswa took measurements of those who were in desperate need of shoes, examined shoes for repair, and enlisted several of the women to help in the work he lined out. With a butcher knife, an awl, and deer tendons for thread, he set about the work, still ranting and cursing the U.S. government.

Over the next several days, the people made clothing, shoes, ammunition pouches, and belts with remarkable skill and artistic flair. The women were patient and calm, yet accomplished much with the material given by old Choswa, who worked diligently on moccasins. When he finished, the women decorated them with beads sewn into patterns long used by our people.

My mother handed me a finished pair she had overlaid with the diamond design my father had had on his deerskin jacket.

I slipped the soft leather over my damaged feet and spread my toes. I was amazed at how perfectly they were made to my size from the crude measurements old Choswa had taken. "They fit."

A little room and give was included for my growth over the next few months. We should be at our new home well before then.

"Yakoke," I said to my mother as I fingered the beaded design.

She stood. "We should not have much further to go. These will take you there, no matter what."

I looked up at her and nodded, trying to understand the concern in her eyes. Or maybe it was just that she was worn out from all the care she gave so many.

I stood and motioned toward the lean-to she had made

for our camp shelter. "Rest. I'll make preparations for the night."

My mother did not heed me as I did not expect her to. She went about doing things that needed doing, despite the fact that I tried to do them for her. If I interrupted her work, she simply moved on to the next task. It wore me out.

When things quieted for the evening, people gathered around fires to tell stories, but many came around me when I opened the book. Nukwia glanced our way but then moved off. To my surprise, old Choswa burrowed his way into the group and sat close to the fire while his hands worked over a leather project. But he listened.

I handed the book to Chilita, who read from a part called First John. Then we talked about the verse that said we were to share our worldly goods with our brothers we saw in need.

I thanked the people there who were always doing such. Chahtas had a giving spirit and we needed to strengthen and build on that and continue to do good in the new land where we were going. In front of the little congregation, I thanked Choswa and the women who had worked to make the journey easier.

Then I looked toward my mother. She sat with a peaceful expression on her face, and I realized how she always was. Always there, in the shadows, in the background, in all the places I needed her to be. She was there to let me know it was right to stand in my father's place. Her love never failed me. She was a mother to many and a wise encourager to my friends.

But I did not say these things in front of the others. My mother would not have it. It would take away from her gentle spirit. So I nodded slightly to her with a little smile.

She understood.

After ending with a prayer, the group dispersed but old Choswa barreled over to me. I started to thank him again for the moccasins, but before I could say a word, he grabbed my leather pouch and cut the string that held it around my neck. I protested and grabbed for the pouch where I had already stowed the book. I could not—would not—let him take it!

He pushed me away with his superior strength but I fought until I felt the warm hands of my mother on my shoulders, tugging me back. I sucked air between my gritted teeth.

Old Choswa yanked the leather string loose from the pouch and proceeded to restring it with the new one in his hand. It was lined with a wide patch of soft leather in the middle. Quick as a swat, he was done and tossed the string over my head. It settled around my neck with the soft patch of leather that would protect my skin, especially as the weather warmed and sweat made it rub and blister.

I stared at old Choswa. He stared back. And then he chuckled. He chuckled and chuckled. Those nearby chuckled. My mother chuckled.

I chuckled.

Chapter Thirteen

I was hard asleep when a hand shook my shoulder. I sat up straight to see Ishtaya in the darkness, finger to his lips to shush any sound I wanted to make.

"Come," he whispered. "We must find Yakni Foi. We fear what he is doing."

I nodded and crawled to my feet, the leather pouch with its new string still around my neck. Nukwia stood behind Chilita, shivering. She nodded toward the trail that led to the river landing. I knew what she meant. I knew where Yakni Foi had gone.

We followed each other through the darkness, sensing our way over the unfamiliar terrain as we went down, down.

The tavern and public house was set far enough from the river to save it from minor flooding in springtime, but close enough to make use of the water for common purposes. The trail we followed came up from the river near the ferry boat. Mist from the river filled the air here, cool and refreshing. But it did not relieve the tension as we climbed the embankment toward the buildings.

Rumors said a touched man by the name of Rorer owned the place. And that he had used the Removal of the Indians to redirect traffic traveling to the Red River country to use his ferry instead of a competitor's upstream. It seemed the whites cheated each other as well, not just the poor savages they considered us to be.

I didn't care about the gossip of the whites, but our people enjoyed telling these stories and poking fun when they could to keep the bitterness and anger at bay. But I knew one person who handled the horrors of it all another way. That was why Ishtaya had awakened me. Why we were walking into a white man's tavern in the middle of the night.

Music and laughter told us not everyone slept. Light streamed from the windows by the tavern door, showing our way up the steps. Ishtaya and Chilita looked to me. Nukwia looked down. I knocked softly and opened the door with hesitation.

It took a moment for my eyes to adjust to the brightness of the room, but I quickly slipped inside with my friends behind me, closing the door without a sound as we gazed around the room. No one noticed us.

The inside was huge, much larger than any structure I'd been in. A fireplace took up most of the far wall, although only coals burned in the late spring night. Near it, a man played a fiddle like Homer's, and like Homer, he seemed limited to one tune, but he played it vigorously as if it was the first time of the evening.

Cots and makeshift beds littered the floors, most along the walls but some blankets were also spread on the large eating table in the center of the room. People curled under these blankets, heads burrowed deep under them in an effort to find some kind of shield against the light and racket of the room.

A man danced about with a jug in hand. He was squatty with plump cheeks, hair slicked over to one side, and a constant grin. Dressed in light colored trousers, he wore a dark vest over his stained white shirt. He went around refilling mugs and tin cups with vile smelling brown liquid. I knew what it smelled like. Enough had been spilled on the floors, all the way to the door.

There were more travelers than I had expected. They must have come in from the east road, from Memphis or somewhere else the whites talked about. We'd heard that once it turned dark, the ferry wouldn't run and travelers would put up here at the public house. I now saw it was as I had feared—more of a tavern than a place to sleep.

The people ranged from hunting parties to more well-bred men that might be on an exploring expedition, maybe heading down to Mexico. I'd heard this was along a suitable route to there.

Some men grew loud from drink, others sat in quiet stupors along the walls, some slept. I was relieved to not see anyone I recognized. At least, not at first.

The man who danced around with the jug, a man I heard someone call Rorer, sauntered over to those sleeping on the table. He flipped back the blanket from the first one's face, took a look and flipped it back. He did the same with the next then went on. I had a chance to glimpse the second face.

Yakni Foi.

There, in the middle of a white man's tavern, passed out on a table, drunk.

I knew there was no reasoning with him, no bringing him to his senses in this condition. I motioned my friends to go out the door. Ishtaya moved to open it. But Nukwia grabbed up a bucket of water by the door and strode forward, dumping the entire pail over the blanket.

A cough and cursing sounded as Yakni Foi tried to disentangle himself from the soggy blanket. Nukwia screeched at him. "Fool! Fool, fool, fool! You hate the white man, despise his wrong ways, yet you are no better than he!"

If Nukwia—shy, timid Nukwia—meant to insult and humiliate her father in the worst possible way, I knew she had succeeded. Yakni Foi didn't blink as he sat on the edge of the table. His hand lashed out, the back striking Nukwia across the face.

I caught her before she fell and Ishtaya put himself between us and Yakni Foi, who tried to get to his feet. Chilita took Nukwia, who was shaking, from me and held her tight.

The music ceased. Rorer made the next move. And move the squatty man did. In three quick steps, he was close enough to seize Yakni Foi by the back of his neck and his waistband. Rorer pushed and dragged the larger man toward the door that another man opened.

Rorer stuck his boot against Yakni Foi's backside and shoved him hard. "'Nuff firewater for you, Indian! Go jump in the river if you want somewhere to drown your sorrows!"

The door slammed and the music resumed. Nukwia cried softly in Chilita's arms, her face turned away from us. Ishtaya looked my way but didn't meet my eyes.

I didn't want to chance an encounter in the dark woods with a drunken Yakni Foi, so I motioned my friends toward the wall furthest away from the fireplace and we settled against it. A long night began.

Chapter Fourteen

The next morning, I awoke to a boot nudging my leg. I looked up to see Rorer above me with a pail of water held high and threatening. I quickly scooted up the wall and to my feet, jostling Ishtaya, Chilita and Nukwia in the process. They awoke instantly and we slipped out the door. The other travelers stirred around and moaned for coffee.

The sun was coming above the trees and I knew we were already missed back in camp. My mother and Tushpatubbee would be disappointed we'd gone off on our own without word. But they would be more disappointed in the man who had caused the night's events.

We didn't say anything as we found the trail by the river to lead us back to our camp. Nukwia's lip was swollen. There was no denying what had happened. I had no words to say. None of us did. We had not done good in the new land as we had pledged to my father's memory.

When we reached camp, I sought out Chief. My mother saw me, but also my determined expression and fell in step with me, Ishtaya, Chilita and Nukwia. Yakni Foi was nowhere in sight.

Most in the camp were about their morning business, finishing with the meal, tending the sick, washing blankets, and settling in for however long we would be here. There was no stir of joy.

We found Chief with a cluster of men, discussing our plan of action, taking inventory of supplies, and assessing the number of sick among us. None of these things were encouraging and I felt guilty for adding to our troubles, but this was important.

At a pause in the conversation, I spoke. "We had trouble last night." I motioned toward Nukwia, who kept her head down but it did not hide her darkened eyes and puffy lips. "We discovered someone missing in the night. We found him in the tavern, drunk and shaming our people."

Tushpatubbee joined the circle then, looking relieved to see us but also troubled. I assumed he'd been looking for us and fearing we may have fallen into trouble.

Chief Baha looked between us. "Who was this man?"

I didn't want to say. I didn't have to. Chilita spoke in a steady voice. "Yakni Foi. Our headman. One who should be an example to us all."

I heard Tushpatubbee sigh, deeply, with sadness that seemed to overcome his own soul. We turned to him.

He had trouble speaking, but finally said in his simple way, "No use worrying about Yakni Foi. Must have fallen in the river drunk. Drowned last night."

Nukwia screamed and collapsed. My mother knelt and held her, Chilita on her other side. Those nearby who heard cried out and moved closer as Tushpatubbee quietly shared how he'd gone looking for us early in the morning and found Yakni Foi on the bank of the river below the ferry crossing. He'd left the body and was returning with the news and for help in carrying our headman back.

I stood in disbelief. I recalled the tavern owner's words, *"Drown your sorrows in the river, Indian."* Had Yakni Foi done just that, or was it truly an accident?

Only Chihowa could know.

Chapter Fifteen

We stayed at the post a long week. Chief Baha believed it would lift everyone's spirits if we started moving again. Surely the trip couldn't take much longer, a few weeks maybe.

Before we broke camp, Ishtaya and I went to Little Rock with Tushpatubbee and several of the men to pick up supplies the Indian agent had set aside for us. We crossed the river on Rorer's horse-drawn ferry and traversed the steep roadway to the town.

Little Rock was the largest white settlement I'd seen, even larger than it had looked from the bluff. Dozens of log structures lined the dirt roads that crisscrossed to make a town. There was a dry goods store, mill, blacksmith shop. There was even a jailhouse.

We circled around town as instructed and soon came to the abandoned military post the Indian agent in North Little Rock said was used as a restock station for the Removal. Fencing enclosed several outbuildings used for wagon repairs, outfitting teamsters, and quarters for those who had joined in the massive efforts to relocate the Indian tribes to the west. But there was little activity here now. The three main Removals had already taken place in previous years. We were part of what was left of our tribe in Mississippi.

When we approached a large storehouse, a man came out the door as if he'd been watching for us. He had a ledger in hand and waved it toward a small pile of sacks and two wood crates. "No need to come in. I got your rations all there, all you were assigned. Now get on, I got things to tend to." The man rested the ledger on his ample waistline and stood there as though we needed supervision to cart off the paltry supplies.

I knew this amount would not see us through the remainder of our journey. But surely Fort Smith, our next destination, would be well stocked to give us supplies before we continued on to Skullyville, our new home fifteen miles from there.

I hefted a sack of cornmeal and put it on my shoulder. None of us had to carry much. The man watched us like we were thieves or beggars. I wanted to tell him of *Nanih Waiya*, the resting place of our ancestors' bones that we had traded for these supplies.

But I took my part of the load in silence as did the others. Even Tushpatubbee had nothing to say as we walked down the rutted road toward Little Rock and the ferry.

Over five hundred whites had already settled in the area. It was disturbing how close they were to our new homeland that President Andrew Jackson promised would be ours as long as the rivers flowed and the grass grew green. *Scoundrel*, old Choswa said.

But that didn't matter now. All that mattered was for our people to get a moving spirit on them, enough to carry us the rest of the way home. Even though going west felt like the wrong direction. Very, very wrong.

Mud, mud, mud turned to sand, sand, sand. The post road we traveled was as dull as the colors beneath my feet. I adjusted the sack of seed corn on my shoulder again. With the trail cutters no longer needed and plenty of hunters, I fell into the simple and mundane tasks of the trail. And nothing was more mundane than walking along with a silent crowd who felt the same way I did.

Along with the gritty sand filling my new moccasins, the sun took its turn tormenting me. In the mornings it teased, slowly ascending with its glare and heat. Summer wasn't fully upon us yet, but that didn't stop the heat from being more than a nuisance to the weary travelers.

And the complaints. Gracious! I never heard so many gripes about stomachaches and fevers and general misery. No one was happy or well that first day we marched on over the sandy post road out of North Little Rock. It seemed no one would ever be happy again.

We settled into camp that evening. While most still felt miserable, there was a feeling of relief that at least we were on the move again, onward, onward to our final destination in Indian country.

But the stomachaches grew worse. I heard a loud wrenching sound in the woods while I gathered kindling for the cooking fires. I peeked through the fading light in the brush and saw a little boy by a bush, vomiting. I backed away and went off to find Attachi, the medicine man.

The boy died two days later from something called dysentery.

Chapter Sixteen

The disease spread quickly through our camp, through the weak and those already suffering from sickness and sadness. Three more among us died in less than a week.

I could not stop thinking of Yakni Foi. I could not stop thinking of all who had died along this trail as we buried our dead in a lonely place near camp. It was lonely, but peaceful and that was comforting to those who came together for the funeral cry. We had not had one since Yakni Foi died and it seemed more was needed than ordinary grief.

Chief Baha said this to me when he asked me to speak words at the cry as my father might have done. I did not want to, did not feel able. But I did feel called.

I stood after the traditional mourning time had quieted. Chilita and Ishtaya stood at my sides. I raised my hands to the sky and prayed. I hoped that was enough.

But then I dropped my hands and looked at my people. I saw Nukwia with unspoken grief clouding her eyes. Keyuchi stared hard at me and Halbi stood with arms crossed. Then I saw my mother, who shared an encouraging word without speaking.

I had to give what I had been given. "We have come so

far since my father revived our spirits and set us on a good path, a path the Great Spirit set us on. But we have seen much sadness and despair, fighting among ourselves. We must serve the purpose of the Great Spirit, each in what he has been called to."

When I paused, no more words coming to me, Chilita spoke. "We have all been called by the Great Spirit, to serve a greater purpose than ourselves. We are being prepared to do His good work. Let us never forget that or those we leave behind to the earth. We must live to do the will of Chihowa if He should find us worthy for service."

Nukwia stepped forward, rubbing her arms with her hands. "Ome."

The band of Chahtas murmured their agreement. No one walked away. I wondered if we would truly become one people again, if we could forget all dissension and despair.

Comforted and encouraged, we worked together and put more effort into reaching our next destination and made excellent time according to what we'd been told. The great dangers of the journey were past and the people were prayerful and filled with hope of seeing the new land soon.

In less than two weeks, we arrived at the ferry crossing at Dardenelle, where we would cross the Arkansas River and make the final leg of our journey to Fort Smith.

The woods broke and we saw the river again. It was wide at this point, but lazy looking. Sandy banks covered both sides of the shore and wooden docks anchored the ferry. Stout ropes held it in place and stretched across the river to the other dock. A wood fence five feet high ran around all four sides of the ferry and a gate for loading was lowered to the dock. A white man and two black slave boys were on the bank. A fire blazed and fish fried in a skillet.

Chief ordered a camp set up while he left to make arrangements for our crossing. To my surprise, he nodded for me to join him, Tushpatubbee and Halbi. We followed Chief down the sandy embankment and he greeted the white man, explaining who we were.

The two boys, who looked to be about fourteen or fifteen, squatted by the fire. They stared up at us. Both were barefoot with pants a season's growth too small and frayed around the edges. Their shirts were ripped and covered with patches, leaving me to wonder why their mothers didn't sew new ones altogether for the amount of material used in patching.

The ferryman spit tobacco and stirred the fish. "I ain't even been paid for the last bunch back when we had to chop ice just to get across each time. Here it is near summer. I ain't about to take on no more Indians with pay promised from that office in North Little Rock. Can't trust them government men for nothing."

When Chief made no reply, Tushpatubbee chuckled softly. "On this, we agree."

The ferryman laughed and Tushpatubbee pulled out his plug of tobacco and offered it to the man.

The conversation progressed quickly and Tushpatubbee obtained the ferryman's agreement to carry us and our possessions across.

Jason, the ferryman, pulled the skillet off the fire and motioned at us. "You likely ain't had nothing to eat since morning. Have a sit down, we got more for the skillet." He barked at the boys, "You two go on and get that other string! Fillet them up good and get them fried. We got hungry men to feed."

The boys scrambled up and ran to the river. They pulled up a string of crappie while we settled around the fire, making conversation through broken English. We learned from the ferryman that several thousand Chahtas had crossed here the past few years. He told of their sad condition, barefoot and nearly naked in the worst winter Arkansas Territory had seen. He saw death when they arrived—death when they left. A terrible thing, he said. But it was none of his doing.

The next morning, Jason and his slaves greeted us and he set about giving orders on how to organize our group and possessions. The crossing would take a few days, he wagered, but it would be easy enough. Spring rains had raised the water levels, but they were no longer at flood stage as they had been a few months ago. Like on the great Mississippi River that had taken my father's life.

I shook myself from such thoughts and helped my mother sort our meager belongings. She smiled at me—it was good to see her smile. I returned it. The weather was so pleasant, the company so cheerful, to do anything less seemed wrong. The journey would be over soon. Everyone sensed it.

I helped Tushpatubbee gather a pile of blankets and load them. But when I set foot on the ferry tethered to the dock, a tremble shot through my leg, shocking me. Surely the fear of a river crossing would not come again? I hadn't felt it at Little Rock on Rorer's ferry. This ferry hardly moved as the river flowed beneath it. It was sturdy and had made countless trips across this river. It was the safest way. Why then, did I not feel safe?

I dropped the blankets on a pile in the corner where Tushpatubbee tied them down. I wrapped the leather pouch in one of them, worrying about the book getting wet again as it often had on this trip. I added my new moccasins, wanting to keep them dry.

I turned and brushed past one of the slaves, who was whistling a bright tune, but I shied away from him. The blacks were more foreign to me than the whites. I had almost grown accustomed to the white's speech and mannerisms. The blacks were different. They jested different, talked different, acted different. When one of the slaves helped me tie a bundle of baskets together, I glanced at him and wondered how else he was different.

Keyuchi pushed between us and scooped up the bundle without a word. All day he had been pushing against me, stepping in and finishing work I had begun. I tried to be patient, but at that moment it took all my concentration not to tackle him, baskets and all. But I let him go and moved on.

The first load ready, I boarded the ferry to help with unloading on the other side. Determined to force away any fear, I wiggled my way between the high load of blankets, baskets, and ropes, and the plank board fence around the ferry. The current of water was only inches away and the splash on my bare feet chilled me.

One of the slaves released the ferry from the dock. He then scrambled on top of a cargo pile and watched the river for trouble spots. The craft dipped and swayed but I kept my eyes up and alert. I put my hand against the load, which was so tall it came all the way up to my chin.

Ten members of our company rode the ferry, anxiously looking to the far shore as we moved into the swift current. I watched the cargo intently, ready to make adjustments if anything slipped. All seemed secure but we couldn't relax.

Midway across I heard something rustling, moving, tumbling near me and turned in time to see the large bundle of baskets sucked away on the downstream current. I felt a jerk as something tightened around my leg. A rope tied to the baskets was looped around my ankle!

I grabbed for the fence, but the current had filled the baskets with water and sucked them down in the strong undertow. The rope yanked me mercilessly to the floor of the ferry. I heard a crack and felt something warm on the back of my head before I was sucked under the bottom plank of the fence and into the chilly waters of the Arkansas River.

The abrupt entry awakened my senses but not enough for me to struggle as the water overtook my body and pulled me under. My arms drifted out from my sides as I flowed along. My leg stretched hard against the rope but it wouldn't let go. I wondered if they would ever find my body. I wondered who would cry at my yaya along the riverbanks.

I wondered if anyone would know I was gone.

A hand gripped my arm. It moved along my body, down

my leg. Then I felt the pressure on my leg give way, surrendering. I was drifting up. Or maybe down. I couldn't tell.

Skin on my skin. Then sandy shores. Then breath where mine should have been and wasn't.

A strong hand slapped my back. More breaths. Finally mine came to me and I gagged. Coughed up half the river.

My head burned and spun out of control and a strange darkness was all I knew.

Chapter Seventeen

My mother held me. I was a baby, helpless in her arms, dependent on her for life itself.

A flash of light, and I held her hand, walked at her side along the trail to the stream. Splashed tiny toes in the water while she laughed.

She laughed.

A flash of light, and I stood on a stump and imitated my father swinging his axe to chop the last of the winter wood. My mother came and gathered me in her arms, scolded me for letting my feet stay in one place in the sleet that had begun. The skin on my soles cracked and bled and I cried.

I cried.

A flash, and my mother held herself on the banks of Bihi Island as she searched the waters with her eyes. She looked at me. She saw my father in me.

She saw.

A flash, and she hummed a lullaby on the banks of the Arkansas River while a fire burned and warmed my skin. She whispered non-words and held me in her bosom.

My mother held me.

I pulled back and opened my eyes to see her face. She

saw my eyes. I burrowed back into her and let my mother hold me while my senses came back.

"How's he doing?" I recognized Tushpatubbee's voice.

"He will be well."

"That slave boy did a good thing. None of us even knew he'd gone under."

My mother hummed and I heard her whisper yakoke to Chihowa. I whispered it as well.

It was long after nightfall before I could sit up and see my friends around my mother's fire. She had propped me against a log and was spoon-feeding me broth before I fully opened my eyes. Ishtaya and Chilita sat across the fire, quiet and watching. Chilita held the book in her hands.

When I finished the broth, I sat up more despite the pain in the back of my skull. It felt as if yellow jackets had built a heavy mud nest there and stung me at will. I swatted at them and moaned.

My mother put her warm hand under my chin and lifted it, looking into my eyes for signs of my condition. I blinked and she nodded. She glanced back at Chilita, who seemed to take that as permission. She opened the book and began to translate from our favorite verse.

The Lord is my Shepherd...

Throughout the verse, I looked around the camp set up on this side of the river. The ferry was on the other side again, tied down for the night. I loathed the thing. It had stolen my sense of security and confidence.

But I tried to listen to Chilita's comforting words, longing for peace to come over me. I relaxed in my mother's arms.

The next morning, I was well enough to feel useless as I was forced to stay in camp and watch the activity around me.

More of our company was brought over, load by ferry load, and I was allowed to help with nothing. That order came from Tushpatubbee, not my mother. I knew she would let me help, no matter how afraid she might be.

I found a fallen tree to sit on near the river and watched as Keyuchi played a hero, being everywhere and helping everyone all at once. He seemed different today, as though he could not do enough good things for the elders, for Chief, for Tushpatubbee. He never once looked my way, but I knew I was the reason he wanted to show out. And there was nothing I could do about it.

Another load came across and as everyone disembarked, I saw the person I needed to see. I jumped to my feet and tried to run, but I was so dizzy I fell to my knees.

I shook my head and carefully stood, walking more slowly toward the docked ferry. As those around me worked, I went up to the slave boy who had climbed on top of the load during the first crossing. The one who had seen me and risked his life to save mine.

"Yakoke," I said to gain his attention. The older boy looked around a moment in surprise before seeing me.

When he did, he grinned with more teeth than I had realized came in a mouth. "Hey there, little Indian. Made it to today still alive and kicking?"

I nodded, studying him. He was really not so different. "Yakoke for saving me. I Tushpa. What your name?"

The boy reached out and pumped my hand. "Ezra. And you's can thank Massa Jason. He the one that give me a knife to carry around and leave to do what I need when we do a crossing. Would no way I could have gotten that rope loose under the current."

"You risked life to save me. Why?"

"Shucks, weren't nothing. I's due for a bath anyway!" Ezra laughed, light and fun. Then he turned serious and put one hand on my shoulder. He pulled me close. "I tell you this. You watch out for that boy that don't like you. He was mighty close around when you went in. Weren't no other way them baskets woulda got loose. You know what I'm saying?"

I did know and a sick feeling was replaced by anger that washed over me with more fury than the river.

I started to turn away, to seek out Keyuchi, but Ezra still gripped my shoulder. "Hold on there, little savage. You ought to know broad daylight ain't the time to get even. You gotta wait til dark. Yes sir." He grinned again, all teeth. "You's nice and dark like I is. You just wait. You have your chance."

I needed to pray. But I didn't. All that day, I didn't tell anyone what Ezra the slave boy told me about Keyuchi. I didn't need to think about how there had been no rope around my feet where I stood guard on the ferry. I didn't need to think about how securely the baskets were tied. I didn't need to think about how Keyuchi's threat had sounded. I didn't need to think about any of it.

But I did. It consumed my thoughts and any prayers I might have said. Keyuchi had tried to *kill* me. And why? Because he thought I'd betrayed my people.

Had I?

The question haunted me above the hate-filled thoughts I had of revenge. Was befriending a white man like Homer betraying my people?

Back in the homeland, many said our leaders were fooled by the whites and had betrayed us to them by signing the Treaty of Dancing Rabbit Creek. They had traded away our homeland, our *Nanih Waiya*, and our souls for peace and a land far away in the West.

Our band had not left in the first three Removals the United States government had planned. Horror stories of the deaths and mistreatment on those trails had circulated in the communities around us, making us more resistant to the move. We held out as long as we could, pleading with our white neighbors to support us, but they said it was none of their doing and there was nothing they could do about it.

So we had prepared. Prepared to weep for our ancestors, to make a four hundred mile journey, to begin a new life in the Indian country where many of our nation had already gone. We brought seed corn, a Bible and hope. These were the most critical to my father.

We still had the seed corn. The Bible. But the hope? Our people were dying. Bickering and betraying one another. My father was dead. Where was the hope to carry us to our new home?

I thought of the whiskey Yakni Foi had drank, drowning his grief. Maybe drowning himself.

Suddenly, he didn't seem so terrible. Neither did Keyuchi. They were my brothers. They did not like all the things I did. I did not like all they did. But we were one people, one nation. And Chihowa created us all.

The Chahtas. The whites. The blacks.

We had to find the overlapping lines between us and live in them. It was up to me to help my people understand this.

So I resolved to let go of my anger. I still would not speak to Keyuchi, but I did not despise him or plot revenge in my heart. I did not yet pray for him; I knew that time would come. For now, I was content to share the words of the book with my people, all who would hear them. To share what I knew with all.

It was enough. For now.

Chapter Eighteen

Once across Jason's ferry, talk among our people of reviving the ball games permeated the camp. Some said we should rest and tend the sick before the remainder of our journey. Others argued the games would lift spirits and give us reason to cheer.

A few turned to me for my stance on the issue. It was those who studied the book who wanted to know. Ishtaya said nothing, but his eyes told the story. He wanted to play the game of our people. It was a way of keeping the past alive, of carrying it into our future. And it was fun. But the vices that too often came with the game were detrimental as my father had admonished.

Tushpatubbee came by the small group of boys and men who lingered around me, no one wanting to ask outright. He paused and looked at me, questioning.

Finally, I gave my answer. "I will play, but only if there is no gambling. My father would not have permitted it. And no drinking white man's whiskey."

We needed something to restore our spirits and connect us to our past, something that would be good exercise and simply fun. So I understood the relief and whoops of excitement that spread around the group when I agreed to play.

Forty men and boys—men and boys who had waded through waist-high swamps, who had suffered hunger and dysentery and had survived, who had buried mothers, fathers, brothers—now ran around like squirrels under a pecan tree, marking off the field and setting up crooked poles at each end.

I took off my moccasins and rushed to help erect a goal post. I borrowed a pair of sticks from Tushpatubbee, who told me to share them when I took a break. Ishtaya had his sticks and a small leather woven ball. We practiced throwing it across the field, diving and catching it with our sticks. Old Choswa tossed three new balls into the fray of practicing players on the field.

We hadn't begun the game, but already, sweat dripped into my eyes and I panted. My head hurt from breathing hard, but I knew no harm could come from running my heart out. It felt good, an immense release through my body.

Then I saw Keyuchi. He was blind to those around him as he darted toward me. Ishtaya flung the ball my direction. I ran to catch it, but one glance at Keyuchi revealed we had the same target. I leaped into the air, sticks positioned for the catch. I snagged the ball on my descent but my feet never touched the ground.

Keyuchi slammed into me as I came down, throwing me backward and causing me to land hard on the earth. My ears rang, eyes watered. My sticks had popped open and Keyuchi scooped the ball and ran for the other side of the field. Ishtaya took off after him. I couldn't move.

Tushpatubbee grabbed my hand and pulled me to my feet. I gathered my sticks and walked off the field, waiting for my vision to clear.

I heard the turkey gobble challenge. The players gathered in the center of the field to pair off into two teams. I blinked and, seeing no more spots, joined them and found myself on a team with Tushpatubbee and Ishtaya, along with several others who often joined in studying the book. Keyuchi was on the other team with Halbi. When the two sides separated, it clarified the two factions in our band.

Playing stickball no longer seemed like a good idea, but it was too late to stop. I realized we now had an audience of more than our own people.

Scattered around the light woods and meadow where the ball field was laid out, several whites mixed in with the crowd that was already swelling, growing loud as onlookers shouted for their teams. The whites had heard about us and had come out from Dardenelle and surrounding farms scattered along the river bottomland.

Paying the crowd no mind, I joined three other players in a circle march as we chanted before the game. These sets of four were scattered around the field as each side chanted for victory.

Chief Baha stood in the center of the field, prepared to toss the ball and start the game. The players spread out, some in defense of the goal posts, others ready to scramble for the ball. A thrill went through me as I prepared, knees bent, to take on the challenge. Rules were already agreed on. The score marker set. The ball was tossed.

With warrior cries, the players rushed forward, slamming into bodies and swinging sticks. In a flash, Tushpatubbee flew down the field toward the goal post, being chased by our opponents.

I ran parallel to him, several feet away, and gave a shout. A player charged Tushpatubbee's shoulder and rammed it, spinning him around. Using the momentum, Tushpatubbee swung his sticks and sent the ball straight toward me.

I caught it and charged toward the goal post, eyeing those who stood guard, watching my every move. My bare feet pounded the dirt and grass and yellow flowers as I darted around players with the goal in sight.

Keyuchi came in from my right. I tried to change course, but another opponent challenged me. Keyuchi gave a shrill call and closed the distance between us.

I glanced his way in time to see Ishtaya throw his sticks

down and tackle Keyuchi.

I spun away from the other player and took aim. I sent the ball shooting from my sticks like a musket ball. Cheers from the sidelines erupted as the ball closed in. But not close enough.

A miss.

I stumbled but turned to chase the ball as an opponent carried it at full speed to the other end of the field. The game had begun.

I took the cool rag off my eyes and tried to focus on the dim light around me. I moaned and turned over, which made me moan again. The blanket door on the shelter flipped back and my mother came in with another rag.

She flopped it on my forehead with a chuckle. "You played well."

"Not well enough," I mumbled but appreciated her praise. I rubbed the rag over my eyes again and around my head, hoping it would ease the pounding there. It helped, but nothing would help my pride over losing the stickball game.

But at least the game had served a purpose in cheering the people and giving an opportunity to show the whites some of our culture. They had thoroughly enjoyed watching the sport.

Whether anyone bet on the game or not, no one said in front of me. No fights had taken place and no serious injuries other than one broken arm. But there were plenty of cuts and bruises to go around. I had my fair share on top of the ache at the base of my skull. Which brought to mind Keyuchi.

How was I not supposed to hate him? Why did the book say such a thing? An enemy was an enemy. Perhaps it wasn't right to hate them, but why did it say we had to love them?

I pushed the warring thoughts aside as I accepted a bowl of corn mush from my mother. "Yakoke."

She seated herself across from me and waited. I knew she

had something important to say. She scrubbed a hand over my head, felt the back of it for heat and swelling. I looked up.

My mother spoke. "You've done much for our people. I am proud of you." Her voice was tired. Her eyes were tired.

It was my turn to feel her head for heat. I frowned. "You should see the medicine man. You are not well."

My mother smiled. It was a good sight. "Well enough to take care of you and your bruises!"

She chuckled and so did I.

Later that evening, gathering wood for an elder's fire, I heard a hacking noise. I followed it soundlessly and spotted Keyuchi in the blackness, bent over double and holding his head.

I debated a moment before slipping away. Sending the medicine man, Attachi, with herbs to help Keyuchi would show something along the lines of love rather than hate. That was a place to begin.

Chapter Nineteen

The next morning we set out again. Ishtaya, Chilita and I walked several paces behind Keyuchi as he staggered and swayed from one side of the road to the other. He bumped into someone, who gave him a steadying hand before moving on. He fell further and further behind the main group. I slowed. So did Ishtaya and Chilita. We said nothing to one another.

Keyuchi dropped to his knees. I kept moving until we were close to him. We stopped. His body trembled and a sheen of sweat covered his back. He held his head as though trying to keep it in place, but his hands were loose, weak. He swayed and toppled toward the ground.

I was closest. I broke his fall and eased him onto the sandy roadside.

"Is he that sick?" Tushpatubbee came back down the road toward us. I nodded. Tushpatubbee felt Keyuchi's forehead with the back of his hand and grunted. He grabbed the boy's wrists and pulled him to his feet before scooping him into his arms. We marched on.

Walked on and on. And on.

Finally, we came to the camp the others had finished

preparing for the night. Attachi, who had treated Keyuchi the night before, saw us and immediately took him to a shelter.

Long after everyone had gone to bed, I stayed up by the last cooking fire still burning. I listened to Keyuchi's quiet moans inside the shelter with the medicine man. He sounded like a dying kitten, pitiful and helpless. His moans wove around me and I knew where they wanted to be, but I blocked them out. He had caused me too much harm.

Forgive.

I shook my head, rubbed a hand over my face, wiped away soot from the fire. I thought of the slave boy, Ezra, and his words. "*Wait til dark. You nice and dark like me. Have your revenge…*"

I could. Attachi would turn Keyuchi's care over to me without question. And if I caused him extra suffering and Keyuchi told, no one would believe it. Or if I mixed the right kind of medicine, he would be able to tell nothing at all.

His moans quieted some, but still floated around me. They bumped into my heart, but I blocked them again. They tried to weave into my soul, but I pushed them back. Then, they whispered to my spirit. *Have pity.*

I reached down to the edge of the fire and rubbed cooled ash between my fingers. I knelt in the ash and used open hands to make great waves, drawing the smoke over my body and my head. I breathed slowly, eyes closed.

Attachi left the shelter in a rush. He and I were the only ones up in the night. I looked to him and he shook his head. He made motions like someone going mad. He shook his head again and walked away.

I stood and went to the closed shelter and pulled back the blanket door. In the light of the dying fire, I looked at Keyuchi, writhing on the bare ground, clutching his stomach and slobbering. He sucked air between his lips and gasped, choked on his own saliva.

It was the most pitiful sight I'd seen. This was not an old man or an old woman who had lived a long, useful life. This was a boy, young like me, taken down to the depths of humanity and humiliation.

I needed no revenge. I didn't want it. The moans pierced my heart along with something else. Compassion. Keyuchi's suffering became mine and I knew I would never be the same.

Slowly, slowly, I knelt by Keyuchi. I put my hands on each side of his head, pushed his hair away from his face and held it. He shivered and opened his eyes. I wasn't sure if he recognized me, but it didn't matter. He closed his eyes, moaned and twisted.

For the rest of the night, I kept cool rags on Keyuchi's forehead and a fire near the shelter, both for light and for warmth.

Right before dawn, the time came.

He'd grown still, all his youthfulness and strength taken. I held his head on my knee, put cool water from a gourd to his lips. I said, "Jesus is the Son of Chihowa. He is the living water. Believe in Him and you will not thirst."

Keyuchi's eyes fluttered. His lips drew tight and I moved the gourd away. He hacked out, "Are you here to avenge yourself?"

I asked simply, "For what?"

He stared at me, glassy eyes wide in pain and disbelief. "I looped the rope around your ankle. You were stupid for not seeing me. Stupid for befriending the whites. I did not wish you death, but would not have regretted…"

He hacked again, eyes squeezed shut as he doubled over, rolling away from me. I tossed away the gourd, took his shoulders and pulled him around to face me. I held his chin with a shaky hand. "Jesus the Christ has forgiven your sins. But you must believe that or it does nothing for you."

He tried to pull away from me, from my stare, but I kept his face near mine. His breath was foul and unbearable, but I held on. "Do you believe this, Keyuchi?"

"Do you forgive me?"

I blinked and my hold wavered. I felt his chin slipping from my hand. I felt his soul slipping into damnation. I tightened my grip. "Yes."

Keyuchi sucked in a deep breath. "Then...I...believe..."

His eyes rolled back and closed. His struggle for air ceased.

Chapter Twenty

We did not walk on the next morning. The sickness spread quickly, leaving many too ill for travel. We made the camp into more than an overnight stay, building shelters, stacking wood. Hunting parties were sent out and others foraged in the woods for healing plants and food. Laughter died on every lip. Only a day's walk outside of Dardenelle, we could go no further.

The water was good here, but the weather grew hot, causing even more suffering. I went out with an exploring party and gazed in wonder at the lush land we found ourselves in. This would make a good home.

Back in camp, I found Chief Baha and Halbi discussing that very point. I slipped over to them, not close enough to join the conversation, but enough to listen in. A few other headmen and Tushpatubbee also closed in to hear.

"We cannot strike a permanent camp." Chief spoke with conviction. "We are still this side of the land promised to us, where our brothers have already gone. It would be wrong."

In a burst of anger, Halbi swept his arm around to indicate our entire camp. "This is wrong! Keyuchi's death was wrong. Yakni Foi's. A dozen others. To be burned out of our homes was wrong! To force our people to march on, even another mile, is wrong. You know this. We cannot go on."

"Yet we cannot remain." Chief spoke quietly. "We would be burned out when more whites come, and they will. Our only recourse, our only hope is to continue on. We will find peace and contentment in the new land when we join our people there."

Halbi turned to Tushpatubbee. "How many new sick are there today?"

Tushpatubbee glanced my way and I saw something in his eyes that made my heart tremble. He stared a long moment, not seeing me. He pushed moist black hair off his forehead and wiped at the sweat there.

The others saw it too, but before any of us could move, Tushpatubbee collapsed.

I thought of Tushpatubbee carrying Keyuchi up the hard, steep road into camp. I saw him carry the youth's body away for burial. I saw the look of sickness in his eyes.

The medicine man tended Tushpatubbee, numbering him with the sick. I sought out my mother as I had not seen her since I went out with the exploring party. She could help tend Tushpatubbee. Her care would revive anyone.

But she was not in our shelter. She was not by the cooking fires. Not caring for an elder.

It was Chilita who found me. Her eyes were sad, filled with tears. I stared at her. "Where is my mother?"

"With the sick, as is my mother."

"I did not see her tending anyone there."

"She is not tending the sick. She is one."

What remained of my world dissipated like the morning mist.

Chapter Twenty-One

In a week's time, another died. But it was not Tushpatubbee. It was not my mother. It was Chilita's.

Halbi and Chilita grieved deeply.

Tushpatubbee recovered, saying it would take more than a little sickness to put him in a grave.

My mother was still not well. She moved slowly among the sick, alternating between being one and tending them. I rarely left her side except when she asked me to fetch water or food or to stop pestering her.

The medicine man had good results from his treatments, and so, with high hopes, Chief Baha ordered the camp be struck though many grumbled that the sick wouldn't be able to make good time. Halbi did not change his stance and before camp was packed, he demanded Chief take a vote and allow the people to decide their own fate.

Chief called the people together, but instead of taking a vote, he announced, "Our supply of parched corn and stores of dried beef and salt are nearly gone. When we reach Fort

Smith, all our needs will be supplied by the United States agent. We are more than fifty miles from there, but we are strong and have come much further. We must go on."

The people in good health grumbled and the sick complained. But the camp was packed and we set out on the road toward that land so far away. I stayed at my mother's side, listened to her pant as we climbed yet another hill. It was good to not walk in mud, but soon, this became its own curse.

My feet found little traction on the sandy road and every step was a scramble either up a hill or down the other side. I could not imagine what the sick ones felt as they tried to walk. And the sun! It burned my scalp through my shaggy hair and made the daytime miserable. Sweat streamed down my mother's face. Her eyes were unfocused, tired. She was tired of walking. We all were.

When we stopped for a rest, I found a spring with cool water and bathed my mother's soft face.

She whispered, "Yakoke," but did not look at me.

Halbi and Chilita came to where we sat on a shaded log. Halbi motioned to me. "Come. I have something we must do. Chilita will tend your mother."

There were few people I would turn the care of my mother over to, but Chilita was one of them. Still, I did not wish to leave her. But Halbi looked intense, insistent. I followed him.

We tramped off the road, through the woods. I didn't know where we were going. I had a feeling Halbi did not know either as he continually changed directions and sometimes paused, looking around at a clearing. We walked for an hour, making a wide half circle and coming back near the road. We topped a hill and saw our people walking, walking. Heads down, spirits low, hearts broken.

Halbi pointed to them. "They are our people. They have suffered too much."

I nodded.

"The Great Spirit could not have intended this misery on us. We have done nothing to deserve this; we have honored our chiefs, though we did not agree with them. But we cannot go on."

As if to emphasize Halbi's point, an elder stumbled and fell to the cruel road below us. Two men tried to help him to his feet, but he waved them away. Finally, they pulled him into the shade and left him to be tended by Attachi. I doubted the elder would ever stand again. He would die, as so many already had and so many more would before this trail ended.

Halbi shook his head. He squatted down in the prairie grass of the hillside. I joined him, continuing to stare at our people, at the sadness. Where was my mother now? Was she still walking or had she been rendered unconscious somewhere? Would the others wait for us to catch up? Could they wait?

Halbi spoke. "This is good land where we stand. You have seen it. Good water, game, farmland. We will plant crops and see a bountiful harvest before the first snows. We will build cabins, and even *chukkas* as we have for hundreds of years, long before the whites knew of us or our ways. Our good ways."

I realized what Halbi had done on our long trek. He had shown me the good land we were in. Had shown me why he wanted to stay where we were.

Halbi's words about our good ways contradicted my father's, his belief that we needed to repent and turn from some of our old ways, from the ways that did not please the Great Spirit.

But now, my father's words seemed hollow. They weren't saving our people. They were all still dying. Keyuchi had. But hadn't the words done good for his soul? I had to believe it.

Halbi wasn't finished. "We will not all die before this trail ends. But we will all have buried a piece of our hearts and souls with the ones we love. Some will bury all of their hearts. I only have my daughter left. You only have your mother."

Halbi stared at me. I felt it, but did not look at him. My mother would not be buried on this trail. She would not. Chihowa would not bring such folly on someone so good. Not when we both had done good.

"We would not be able to see their graves again, to perform our funeral cries over them. How many of us will be able to visit the graves of the ones we love? None! They are lost to us."

I nodded, numb, unable to reason Halbi's words in my mind, but somehow, I believed him.

"Tushpa, you have influence among our people, and with Chief Baha. I will call a council tonight. Will you speak the right words to them?"

I nodded, not knowing what I was committing to, only that something had to be done, something none of us would agree on.

Halbi clamped my shoulder and nodded. "You are a good Chahta."

I had to go back over the road at least a mile before I found my mother and Chilita. Ishtaya and Nukwia had joined them. They helped my mother along. She needed it.

Her feet dragged on every step for she couldn't lift them. Ishtaya was under one of her arms, supporting her, Chilita under the other. Nukwia led the way, a gourd of water in one hand and a damp rag in the other.

Nukwia scowled at me when I approached. "Your mother needs you."

I ignored her stare and went straight to my mother, who had paused and was trying to breathe. "Mother."

She looked up at me. Smiled. She had begun to smile more, even on this trail, than ever before.

I did not understand why, especially now. "You should rest. We will catch up with the others when they make camp."

More sick were behind us on the road. It would be late before we were all together again. I didn't care. I only wanted my mother to be whole and well again, in body and in spirit. But I couldn't help her, except in one way. To speak out with

Halbi against the guidance of our chief and what my father had commissioned us to do before he died.

My mother would not rest. Without a word, she continued up the hill. I got behind her, put a supporting hand on her back and pushed as gently as I could with my small strength.

There was such a long way to go.

Chapter Twenty-Two

The cooking fires still blazed when we arrived. I noted Halbi leading a few other men in making shelters for the sick. Shelters that looked more permanent than those needed for an overnight stay. Chief Baha seemed to note this as well, but said nothing as the little group around my mother passed him.

I helped my mother into a shelter and lowered her to the ground. Chilita and Nukwia shooed me away, saying they would tend her feminine needs.

Before leaving, my mother took my hand in her weak one. "We must go on." This was all she said before letting her head rest on the ground, eyes closed.

I heard the call for the council. Halbi pointed his chin at me when he walked by, and joined the group around the main fire.

More Chahtas closed in around the council. Tushpatubbee sat off to the side, smoking his pipe while he skinned a squirrel. Old Choswa seemed to ignore the council entirely as he worked over a hide by another fire. But I recognized the tilt of his head. He listened.

Ishtaya stood by my side as I waited, arms folded over

the leather pouch, feeling the pound of my heart through it.

Chief acknowledged Halbi without speaking first. It was up to Halbi to convince the others of his plan. Chief had had his say the night before.

Halbi looked around the circle and at those beyond in the faint twilight. He summarized his plan of ending the long walk of death and despair, of settling where we were, of making a home at last. Many listened to him, growing more vocal as he spoke. A few raised fists and shouted to end this trail of tears.

Halbi looked at me. I knew what he expected. I knew what my father had expected. My mother. Everyone. No one agreed what the right thing was.

We could not stay. That would violate our word to move to the new land peacefully. But we could not go on. My mother was dying.

Dishonor or death. That was a grave choice to lay at the feet of a youth. But it was not my decision. I would bear no real blame or praise.

I motioned to Chief. "My father would say go on. I would say stay or see more death. The Great Spirit charges us to do good, live peaceably and honor our word. Yet so much suffering. I cannot say either of you is right." I left off there, afraid to say more. Making no unifying proclamation might be a detriment, but far less than speaking from my lack of wisdom.

As the discussion heated and escalated, Chilita stepped forward and raised her hands for silence. The council turned to her.

She spoke in a strong voice, looking at her father first. "My father is right. The sick cannot go on to the new land with no provisions, no rest." Half the people shouted their agreement, echoing her words. Then she turned to Chief Baha. "Chief is right. We cannot settle on land that is not ours. We must honor our chiefs' word."

Some grumbled and spit but others nodded.

I wondered at the wise Chilita, how brave and clear she spoke. But what she had said did not offer a solution. Her next words did. "We must divide into two groups. The ones in good health must go on to the new land, fulfill the word of our chiefs. Some can return with help and provisions for the sick to make the balance of the journey."

Before she finished speaking, a roar of disapproval sounded from both sides as they shook their heads and made protests.

Halbi glared at his daughter. "We will not separate. We are as one family now."

"We leave no one behind! We will die together!"

"We must all go!"

"We will all stay!"

I moved close to Chief and whispered a suggestion. He nodded and moved to the center of the arguing people. "We will cast ballots for who will stay and who must go on to the new land. Fifty will go—the remainder will stay and tend the sick. This is the only way."

More complaints and arguing followed, but finally, twenty-five separated off as willing to make the remainder of the march. The rest could not agree, so Chief cast the ballot. He urged those to whom it had fallen to take their leave first thing in the morning, moving on at a good pace to the new land. There was contention, but gradually all agreed to heed the lot fallen to them.

Except me. It fell on me to go.

I stared at Chief, sudden defiance and determination sweeping through me. I had suggested the ballot cast without thought to the consequences, but that did not hold me now. I had earned the right to make my own decision. I prepared to refuse.

Tushpatubbee came to my side. "Tushpa, Halbi has been elected to move on with his family. He's honoring our old way of casting ballots and not questioning the outcome. You know you have to. You can't go against our old ways in this, or we can't part peacefully as a family. Show them how to do good, no matter what."

I shook my head. "I will not leave my mother! My duty is

to her."

Tushpatubbee shook his head. "I'm supposed to stay behind. I'll look out for her. I adopted you as my nephew when your father died. You've been wise in listening, and I've learned things from you. But listen to me now. You have to abide or every good thing you've done for our people will have been for nothing."

His words were true. I knew that before he spoke. But I feared if I left my mother, I would never see her again.

I looked around at our people, many already wailing, saying farewells and preparing for an early morning departure. We all knew. We would never see one another again. Alive. We had come so far, endured so much, borne so much on one another's shoulders. Now it all ended. What would the next venture in life hold for those who survived? Very little in my mind.

"Say your parting words, Tushpa. You don't want to wake your mother in the morning."

Chapter Twenty-Three

When I went to the sick shelters, I found my mother sipping soup with the help of Nukwia. The girl's lot had fallen to remain in the camp along with others, including Ishtaya and his family.

I crawled on my hands and knees in the low shelter to my mother's side.

"It hurts," she moaned, her eyes drifting closed.

I put a hand on her forehead. "I will be back very, very soon. We are going for supplies. You rest." I glanced at Nukwia with a question in my eyes. She nodded her agreement.

"Nukwia will care for you until I return. I will be back very, very soon."

My mother whispered something. I leaned close to her lips and she repeated, "*Chi pisa la chike.*"

I took her hand and squeezed it. I pulled away, walked into the woods and cried.

Ishtaya saw off those of us going on down the long road. He gripped my forearm and his eyes blazed with light. "We will take care of them. Every night, I will say what verses I can remember to comfort the sick and those working to save them. We must not stop."

I realized I was looking up slightly at Ishtaya. He'd had a growth spurt ahead of me, and he had more the look of a man than a boy.

I gripped his arm in return. "We will be back very soon."

Ishtaya nodded and stepped back when Tushpatubbee came to me. He handed over a familiar knife case. "I don't think Keyuchi would mind you having it. I was going to give it to you when we all got to Skullyville, but…well, you might need it along the way."

I knew what he hadn't said. He didn't know if we would see one another again. If death would claim one or both of us before then. If I would make it to Fort Smith. If I would make it back.

I took the knife and nodded firmly to both my friends. "Chi pisa la chike. I will see you again. Very soon."

I turned away, hesitated, then turned back, lifting the string of the leather pouch over my head. I handed the pouch to Ishtaya, who took it with surprise. I said nothing more as I walked away.

We marched at the fastest pace we had set during the journey. There was an urgency we hadn't assumed before. All traveling were in good health, and the thought of ending our long journey drove us on toward that oft thought of place— Fort Smith and Indian country. Several weeks ago, we thought it not far away. I didn't trust how far it might be now. It was too far for immediate help. My mother was ill. We had to hurry.

We walked until dark, setting up a quick camp in the moonlight. Halbi had not looked my direction since the evening before. If it was only that I hadn't spoken in favor of his plan, it might have been dismissed. But I also swayed his daughter in ways he did not understand nor did he want to. He did not accept the gospel we shared, insisting it was white man's religion and the white man's God. That He was not the same as our Great Spirit, the Creator.

We set a brisk pace the next morning, although few of us had eaten. We'd left most of the provisions with the sick and pushed on with little more than desperation and hope to feed us. We filled our stomachs with cool spring water and bedded down as soon as possible when night came again, hoping to find relief from hunger in our sleep.

The next day we passed white farms. A large garden stood near the fence of one. A woman paused her hoeing to watch us as we passed—a ragged lot of fifty poorly clad Indians, faces drawn from lack of nourishment and the shadow of death and disease on every face.

The two children my father had saved from drowning in the river stood by the fence and stared at the lush red tomatoes on the vines. But they made no move to take one, although the smaller of the two put his hand on the fence.

The woman dropped her hoe and came over. She plucked off a handful of tomatoes and handed them to the children. She pulled string beans from their vines and passed them to the mother who had come to collect her children. The mother dipped her head in thanks as others from the group ventured toward the fence.

The woman looked alarmed, but when she glanced between her bountiful garden and the starving Indians, she set about pulling what fruit and vegetables were ripe enough for eating and passed them over the fence to my people.

I begrudged even this slight delay, not wanting to lose a moment of precious time when it could mean life or death for my mother. But when the others moved on, I found myself going over to the woman to see what she had left.

She turned and saw me. I knew the sight I must look.

The image of a heathen savage with my ragged clothing and dirty feet. My moccasins dangled around my neck as I let my feet feel the earth and stay connected to the life around me. And I needed something to replace the hollowness the lack of the leather pouch had left me with.

The woman held out her palm with three string beans—all she had left from her vines. She'd picked them clean.

She'd given what she could. I gladly accepted them.

I wanted to give her something, but what did I have to offer? I felt the press of the knife in the leather pouch on my belt. Tushpatubbee said I might need it along the way. He was right. I took the case off and offered it to the woman.

Her eyes widened but she shook her head. "You may need that, you poor soul. Keep going. You're almost to the fort."

The words encouraged me and my eyes fell in shame for every evil thought I'd had toward whites. I lifted my eyes to hers and nodded. "Thank you." She looked surprised by my use of English, but perhaps more so by my next words. "God bless for your kindness. I pray blessings for your home."

I turned and walked on to catch up with my people. I heard her call behind me, "God be with you all, and bless your souls."

Chapter Twenty-Four

We were blessed. Before the day ended, we came in sight of Fort Smith, Arkansas Territory.

Someone in our party whooped with joy. We hurried on, nearly breaking into a run despite fatigue and near starvation during our fifty mile trek from the sick camp.

Chief Baha slowed our pace and led the way into the fort. His red turban was situated over his black hair that had grown more white with each mile of our journey. He held his head high, and we followed his example, though anxious about what to do next. I was the most anxious, the spirits of those we'd left behind constantly with me, whispering of the desperate situation.

To our surprise, some relatives of those in our party were at the fort. They'd gotten word a band of Chahtas was coming and they traveled there in hopes of seeing their loved ones again.

The joyous reunions made my heart ache for my mother and also for my cousins and aunts and uncles and others who had come before us. None of them were in this group. None there to greet me nor many of the others. But still, there was a revived spirit and plans were made.

I went up to Chief Baha, who was conversing with Halbi. I heard Chief say, "Skullyville is but fifteen miles from here. Once I have attended everyone safely there, I will hurry back to the camp with provisions. Perhaps a wagon or two can be obtained here."

I interrupted. "We must go back, now! Time cannot be taken to see the rest on to Indian country. We have to get supplies and move!"

Chief looked at me with disapproval, but it faded when he saw the fear and redness in my eyes.

Halbi spoke next. "You go, Chief. Tushpa, Chilita, and I will make arrangements for wagons and all the supplies the captain will give us. We will start the journey back. You can catch up with us on horseback. The wagons will be slow, and the trip back is fifty miles."

I looked at Halbi with gratitude.

The next morning, on full stomachs and with supplies, the main party, led by Chief Baja, left Fort Smith. They headed for our final destination of Skullyville, Indian country.

I couldn't think about the people going on to Indian country without me. I couldn't think of leaving more of them behind. How much would this trail separate and destroy us?

Halbi continued to haggle with the agent in charge to obtain supplies and two wagons for the journey back to the sick camp near Dardenelle. I grew impatient with the debates and Halbi was worse. He did not like being among whites, especially those who looked at us with suspicion or contempt. They didn't seem to trust our word that we were going back to help those in the sick camp.

Chilita ignored those whites and admonished us to do the same. Since her mother's death, Chilita had grown bolder than ever. She quoted verses to her father's displeasure and my chagrin.

I no longer had the book. Didn't know if I would see it

again. If my mother didn't survive this journey as my father hadn't, what good would any of it be? What was the good I had done as my father charged us all to do?

Finally, all was in place and the three of us began the journey back. I drove one of the wagons. It was not a new experience for me, as some of our neighbors back in Mississippi had wagons and my father taught me to drive them so I could be greater help in harvest time. But these wagons were large and cumbersome, with their white bonnets and team of four horses. I kept my wagon close behind Halbi, who thankfully set a good pace with Chilita on the spring seat beside him.

It suddenly occurred to me that Halbi was not responsible to be there at all. He had no relatives back in the sick camp. Yes, he was a headman, but all the others had continued into Indian country with Chief Baha. Some would return to help, but Halbi had never been asked, and yet he never seemed to have considered doing otherwise.

I respected the man more than I had during the entire journey and thanked Chihowa for the headman's leadership. Perhaps I could be such a leader someday. I would set my heart and mind to the task.

But first, we had to travel back and see if my mother lived or had died.

Chapter Twenty-Five

A storm stirred on the horizon behind us. This was our third day of traveling back to the sick, and the storm had arisen in the afternoon, casting a strange darkness for a sunny time of day. But then, nothing along this journey had been predictable.

Lightning bolts shot through the sky before me, followed by great booms of thunder, terrifying the horses. Terrifying me, which made them doubly afraid.

The horses skittered toward the side of the road. I leaned back on the reins, trying to get my team to follow Halbi's wagon, but this only caused them to stop completely. The wagon was dangerously close to the drop-off that fell away from the road.

I wanted to curse the team, curse Halbi who disappeared over a rise in the road, curse the soldiers at Fort Smith for giving us an addled team of horses.

Then I thought of the white woman whose farm we had passed, of how she had stripped her garden clean to feed us and then had called us poor and had blessed us. Poor we were. Blessed?

Blessed are the poor in spirit, for theirs is the kingdom of heaven.

The words came without me having to recall them. Perhaps we were blessed, but at this point, frustration was winning out on all accounts.

I eased the team forward with light urging. Dark clouds overtook us and opened up. Rain stung my eyes, but I could still make out my skittish team that pranced close to the edge of the road.

A flash of lightning revealed an opening in the trees and I could see the precipice we passed, a long, tumbling slope of rocks and destruction.

I yanked back on the reins. One of the lead horses reared against the bit. I tried to hold the team still, hold them steady while I got my wits about me, but they would have none of it. They jerked forward in the harness and bolted closer to the edge. With a sickening creak of the wagon, the right front wheel dropped off the road.

The jolt sent me flying from my seat. I hit the rump of a horse, breaking my fall but making my descent no less terrifying as I landed amidst the rocky decline. I rolled to a stop against a boulder.

The horses above me on the road reared again. I pulled myself to a sitting position as rain poured over my cuts and bruises, numbing the injuries.

With fierce determination, I scrambled up the incline to the wagon and hauled myself onto the precariously tipped seat. I grabbed the reins and shouted at the team, urging them forward. But they did not pull the wagon back onto the road. Instead, they dragged the right back wheel over the edge as well.

I knew the wagon was about to tip and I would die. I had done no good for my people, my mother, the Great Spirit.

"Chihowa!"

Thunder boomed in answer, a bolt of lightning blinding my eyes. Then someone stood at the head of my team. At first I thought it was an angel, or maybe Christ Himself.

But this form was familiar to me as was the voice I heard soothing the team with Chahta words. He led them back onto the road with gentle urging.

Chief Baha.

I slumped on the seat, my head suddenly throbbing. I had hit it in my fall, but paid it no mind. Now it demanded my attention, my focus.

In the eerie light of the afternoon storm, I saw Halbi top the hill on foot before us. He paused and waited until we drew even.

He and Chief conversed a moment, then Halbi went back to his wagon, which was stopped not far down the road ahead of us.

Chief tied his horse to the back of my wagon and joined me on the seat. He gave me a helping hand and little shove to send me tumbling into the back of the wagon. Maybe it was because he knew I was injured that he sent me back there. Maybe it was because he thought I was still too much a boy to handle the rest of this journey.

I didn't care which it was. I curled up in the bed of the wagon amidst the supply of blankets and rations we had brought from Fort Smith. I lay in a ball, arms wrapped around my knees, praying thanks to Chihowa that I was blessed and filled with renewed hope for the survival of my people.

I was blessed.

Chapter Twenty-Six

The storm eased that evening and the next day, but lingered with us. We set as fast a pace as we could over the slick road that challenged our every step. At one point, we had to unload both wagons and drive the teams from the ground to crest a particularly wicked hill.

Chilita and I worked alongside each other, both quiet and thinking on the ones in camp or the ones who had gone on to our new home. Or maybe she thought only of her mother as I thought of mine.

We made a late camp and I set myself to tending the horses. Our band had no horses to bring from Mississippi, so this was a new chore along the trail.

The soldiers had given us feed sacks and plenty of grain for their animals to be well cared for. I measured and filled the sacks before strapping them over each muzzle as instructed. I watered and groomed the horses, petted and whispered bribes to them to keep a sturdy pace on the difficult road. My mother's life depended on it. I had to believe she was still alive.

The next morning, we set out under the threat of a new storm. This was a lazy one, content with teasing of its coming fury with silent lightning bolts across the sky behind us. I ignored the threats as I rode alongside the wagon on the horse Chief Baha had brought from the fort.

When I recalled the hundreds of miles my people had walked, riding made me feel guilty. Yet riding wasn't easy and I soon became sore in certain areas. I gave up and walked the slick road, leading the horse along with me.

I recognized the next hill. When we left the camp, I had often looked back at this hill, as long as it was in sight. The sick camp lay on the other side of it.

At the crest, in the trees, someone watched. It was Ishtaya. He walked to us, slowly. Too slowly. His eyes were cloudy, his lips pulled tight, face pale.

He answered the question in my eyes. "Your mother lives. She has Chihowa with her. The rest are going mad."

Ishtaya and I went to my mother first while Chief and Halbi saw to the rest of the people. Tushpatubbee was with her. Nukwia was not in sight and I wondered if she were among the eight Ishtaya said had perished in our absence. The number was staggering considering the small party.

My mother lay in a shelter on a bed of soft leaves and blankets, wrapped securely and with care near a low fire. In the heat of early summer, she shivered with sweat beads above her lips. Her eyes opened when Tushpatubbee moved away and allowed me to kneel at her side.

I took her hand and she nodded. "It has been good for me here. I have read from the book. I found great truths."

I held her hand. "We are doing good and will do good. We will be a worthy people for Chihowa."

At this, she shook her head. "We are not good. We are not."

Her words crushed me. All I had done, all I had sacrificed and stood for, it was as I feared. All was for naught. We were a condemned people without hope.

But my mother wasn't finished. She looked to Chilita and

Ishtaya, who knelt by me. "Read. Read that verse."

Ishtaya seemed to understand. He removed the leather pouch from around his neck and withdrew the tattered book. The pages seemed so frail and tender, yet strong beyond my comprehension. As my mother was.

He handed the book, opened to a marked passage, to Chilita. The passage had been marked before the book came into my hands so long ago.

Chilita translated, "Why do you call Me good? None is good except the Father."

Odd warmth spread from my mother's hand through my body. "Do you see, Tushpa? He is the only good. But if He is with us, He is our good. Jesus the Christ is our good."

She coughed. Her eyes drifted closed and sounds of sleep came.

I laid her hand softly under the blanket and rose. Chilita stayed by her side while Tushpatubbee and Ishtaya joined me in the coming darkness of the storm and evening.

Chief and Halbi came to us. "Fear and panic are consuming the people." A wail rose from the woods, followed by another.

Tushpatubbee said, "They believe an evil spirit followed us and now wants to torment us to death. That we're accursed and need to make some kind of sacrifice to remove the curse."

Ishtaya added, "They believe the spirit wants to smite us before we have a chance to enjoy happiness and pleasure in the new land. Fear is all they know."

I looked around the random fires where sick and well alike sat huddled, some wrapped in blankets, some nearly stripped bare with ash covering their bodies as they moaned. I searched each face for hope. There was none.

Halbi muttered, "A civilized people should know better." He looked at me. "You must tell them."

Ishtaya, who had the book and leather pouch in hand, passed them to me. I took them and spoke in a loud voice, gaining a surprising amount of attention. "Brethren, my family! This evil, this sickness on us is not from an evil spirit nor punishment from the Great Spirit, our Creator. He has not abandoned us, not from the beginning of time. He has done us good, a good we cannot begin to deserve. No man can; red, white or black. We can only accept it. We can only believe. Believe on the name of the Lord Jesus Christ and you will be saved!"

All who were able rose to their feet and waved hands through the air, crying out. Crying.

Thunder clapped and lightning flashed over us. The rain came. Poured over our heads, washed away the dirt, the grime, the ash.

I raised my face toward the heavens and spread out my hands, holding the book covered by the leather pouch. "Be our good Chihowa! We receive you now as our children will."

Shouts of agreement from the people echoed my words.

Ishtaya said, "Ome."

I was almost certain I heard Halbi whisper it too.

After a moment of silence, I turned to Tushpatubbee. "Where is Nukwia?"

He removed his coonskin hat and let water from the healing rain pound his bare head, slicking his long, scraggly black hair down over his eyes. He bowed his head and shook it. "Some thought she was a curse on our people because of her father. They drove her away while I was out hunting. Someone found her at the bottom of a ravine. Broken neck. No knowing or saying for sure what happened."

The rain poured down my face, joining with any tears that might have been there. I returned to my mother's bedside.

Chapter Twenty-Seven

The storm continued, angry and relentless. Ishtaya, Chilita, and I worked to secure the shelter as best we could to keep it warm and dry around my mother. Halbi, Chief Baha, Tushpatubbee and others who were well enough made the sick comfortable and fed them broth.

My mother ate nothing.

That night, she raised up, eyes wider than I had ever seen them. She looked around at us, seeing and not seeing.

Her hands moved through the air as she spoke. "I had a vision! Tushpa, you will yet be a good and great man, you will do many things for our people. Ishtaya was there. Chilita, you will be the mother of great men whose deeds you will be unable to number. You must all love Chihowa who took Kanchi from the waters of the great river. Kanchi has been our guardian angel on this journey. Chihowa will see us through the rest of the journey; the sick will recover and be happy in the new land."

She collapsed back. I lifted her head, held her in my lap.

I held her.

Chilita and Ishtaya called for the others. Her friends gathered, crowding around her bed.

My mother's eyes flickered, light catching and shining from them. "My death is near. You must not be afraid. The Great Spirit is yet with us and will always remain with those who sacrifice to be His good in the world. Do not be afraid…He is with us always…"

Her face lit up as one who sees no death but life. She saw more than we could comprehend. She laughed and smiled.

My mother smiled.

She breathed her last breath on this earth.

Some marveled at such wise words coming from the dying. Some believed her prophesy of the sick recovering, and her vision of Kanchi being our guardian angel. Some felt the loss so deeply, they could say nothing.

I was none of those.

I held my mother's body close, felt her spirit move around me and through me and I wept for her.

I wept.

Chihowa is with us. This was believed by all who remained of our company still trying to reach our new home. There was a hopeful spirit in spite of the grief as we buried our dead.

I tried to find that hope, but the sight of Nukwia's grave haunted me. Yet I had done all I could for her and her father. I wanted to believe that. Someday.

But today began as our long journey had, before we left our homes, when we gathered to have a cry for our land, for our way of life. It was good to bury some of the old ways, the superstitions. I knew this at Nukwia's grave. But it was good to keep some of the old ways, in being a strong and adaptive people. I knew this at the grave of my mother.

After the cry, we continued to attend the sick. They made fast recovery with the new hope flooding through the camp as the spirit of darkness and despair evaporated with each morning sun. Hope rose with the dawn.

A week later, still grieving but in better spirits, we prepared to strike camp. The sick had miraculously recovered as my mother predicted, and I wondered if her other predictions would come true. That my friends and I would live to see adulthood, do great things for our people. Only that unconquerable foe—time—would tell. But even it rested in the hands of Chihowa.

On the last night in camp, Ishtaya, Chilita and I gathered without anyone suggesting it. We went to her grave in a peaceful grove of Arkansas pines. It pained me that she was buried here, her grave so far from our new home.

Her grave was well marked with the stones we'd gathered and lined it with. A wooden cross like the missionaries used to mark graves stood at her head.

Chilita spoke first. "I pledge, on this grave of my friend, to live a worthy life, one devoted to Chihowa."

Ishtaya said, "I promise to live a life of usefulness, one who does nothing outside the will of Chihowa."

I wiped at the tears in my eyes, unable to speak at first. Finally, I whispered, "Chi hullo li. Chi pisa la chike. I will come here again."

I pulled the moccasins off my feet. I fingered the beaded diamond pattern across the top, already worn from the hard trail but still showing the care and dedication she had used in the design. I placed the moccasins by the cross as a gift to her memory, to honor what she had done in my life.

Ishtaya removed the beaded belt he wore, kissed it and laid it on her grave. "The gift you gave me, I give to you."

Chilita held a small bowl in both hands and carefully laid it on the grave. "This bowl you carried from our homeland, made from the clay that held the bones of our ancestors. It belongs with you always."

The tears did not stop for any of us, so we knelt together by the graveside, murmuring words of encouragement, sadness and hope, remembering the many things she had done for our people and for us. I pledged to return to her someday.

Chi pisa la chike. I will return.

And in my spirit, I knew I would someday see her face-to-face in the presence of Chihowa.

Weary, emaciated, penniless but with hopeful spirits, our remnant of the devoted company reached Indian country at last and joined our friends and relatives at Skullyville. There was great rejoicing and even I found occasion to smile at the reunion and gaiety of the gathering as stories were shared, tears cried, food prepared and laughter began.

So ended our four hundred mile journey, the most tragic and wonderful event of my lifetime.

Tushpa's Story Continues...

Not long after we joined the others at Skullyville, my people, so long together and seeing much death and destruction as one family, separated from each other. I traveled with a small group going west, to where my mother's relatives had settled. I joined them there, memories of parting with my friends a constant heartache, but my family assured me we would all see one another at gatherings and church.

Ishtaya lived east of Skullyville and in one of our visits together, he told me of his desire to become a preacher. He had grown into a man, strong in faith and body. A new twinkle had formed in his eye and he often told jokes and in general made people feel good and welcome.

I was not surprised to see the young woman Chilita had grown into nor did it shock me when, at age, she and Ishtaya married. He had taken a white name, Willis Folsom, and they settled down together to see if more of my mother's prophesy might come to pass and they would see many great and godly children. I had little doubt of this.

I moved to San Bois Creek area and raised stock.

Our people were at peace and living in fulfillment for

many years. Then war came.

I had never wanted to cause death. Yet I answered the call when it came to defend our territory against northern aggressors. This was the way we viewed those in blue coats, since the United States government had abandoned its promise to protect and defend us from all enemies. When the U.S. soldiers vacated the forts that had stood since my people migrated to Indian Territory, the whites south of us in Texas and also in Arkansas threatened to invade our lands if we did not ally with the Confederacy.

Many of the tribes argued and fought over which side to take. Families divided. Tribes were in an uproar. In the end, the Choctaw Nation and several other tribes decided to align with the South while others sympathized with the North.

My patriotic duty called me to join the Jackson McCurtain Choctaw Company and defend our new homeland against the enemy. This meant doing what I did at Poison Springs, Arkansas—kill. The battle was fierce. Many Indians died there.

My company was on the border of Arkansas, near where it joined Indian Territory.

I knew. I had been here before.

The memory of cannon fire still rang in my ears, along with countless bullets whizzing around me. These memories would not allow me to sleep. Screams of men dying, of ones I killed, haunted every waking moment.

I slipped away in the dark of night and found the seldom used road leading out of Dardenelle. Much of the country had changed in the nearly thirty years since I last traversed these hills. Sturdy oaks grew in what had previously been meadows. Countless farms took up much of the view.

Near dawn, I abandoned the road and found my way over a bluff and then another. I remembered.

I remembered Halbi taking me through these woods. I

thought of the aged warrior and how Chilita told of his conversion before he died of a fever the previous winter.

With the first rays of dawn, I found the well-marked grave. It too had changed. Sunk in and the rocks buried beneath years of mud from rain, and the cross had long since returned to the earth as dust along with the gift we had left.

I settled near the grave, thinking over my life since that long, long walk. It had shaped the man I'd become. I remembered the leather pouch almost constantly around my neck on the trip. I still kept the Word close, although I had stored the original book away and obtained a new one from my church. The verses had sustained me.

The flood of memories reminded me of how close Chihowa had felt then. I had depended on Him for every breath, every step and stumble through swamps, over and in the rivers, through the white man's territory, through the fights and dissension among my people. Chihowa had seemed too distant at times, even cruel.

Yet I knew now He had been my constant companion and strength, guiding my way as I struggled to live my father's example of sharing what he'd been given. I had blamed Chihowa for taking my father and later, my mother. But all these things—tragic and harsh as they were—ultimately had been used for good in my life. And in the lives I touched and that touched mine.

I pondered these thoughts as the sun rose and circled slowly across the sky until it came to the point of setting. I looked at it, looked west to my home. Tushpatubbee had told me to always look toward the sunset, keep my head up and look toward my new home. I never forgot that and often watched the sun set over my home and remembered his words and the many sunsets we walked into during the four-month journey. Many never lived to see the sun set in the new land. This made me doubly sure to lead the kind of life I was admonished to and honor their spirits.

I rose and stood over my mother's grave. "Chi pisa la chike. I promised to return and I have. And I will see your face again someday. The Father is good."

The most prized possession on my person was the bayonet on my rifle. I removed the costly piece and thrust it deep in the ground as a headstone for the grave. Leaving something of value was according to our old custom as a sign of devotion to her and this sacred place. Some of the old ways were still good ways.

I contracted smallpox during the war and was sent to the hospital at Fort Towson, Indian Territory. I was enrolled under the name of John Culberson. I accepted this as inevitable and never went by Tushpa again.

After I recovered, I stayed on at the hospital as a helper. I much preferred helping men recover to killing them.

In this strange place, I learned to read.

When the war ended, I returned to Skullyville to find work. I was industrious and known as a good Christian man, which I took in stride. I knew what "good" meant.

I attended church and Sunday school regularly and was a devoted church worker. Since learning to read the scriptures for myself, I began teaching Sunday school classes.

Then it happened.

At one of these services, I met her. The daughter of the village blacksmith. Lucy McDonald.

In 1868, we were married in Skullyville by none other than Ishtaya, otherwise known as the Reverend Willis Folsom.

Lucy and I settled on a farm just southwest of Skullyville and enjoyed a peaceful, content life. We hosted many travelers and friends. Someone was always in need, and no one was turned away no matter their race or creed. The Culberson home became known for its charity and love, to the white and the black and the red. And to the widow and the orphan as commanded in scripture.

Our fireside was often visited by Ishtaya and Chilita when he had an appointment to preach nearby. Sometimes we would visit the Folsom home. What good times we had!

We almost forgot all the horrors and tragedy on that trail so long ago until someone brought them afresh to our minds. But along with them, the better memories as well.

Lucy heard the dogs braying while I was off hunting. A call came from outside.

"Culberson *mutte*? Where is Culberson?"

She opened the door to see the older man standing on the steps. He did not attempt English, but she realized he must be a friend and invited him in, motioning to the chair near the roaring fire.

He spoke his name at last. "Johnson Bond."

He was dressed in the garb of a woodsman with a hunting coat of various colored yarn woven in, buckskin breeches and beaded shot pouch. His powder horn and rifle lay on the floor beside him as he waited.

I soon returned and caught sight of him. I shouted with joy as I hadn't done since boyhood. "Tushpatubbee! Halito! *Chim achukma*?"

My uncle stood with a grin and we embraced. We rattled away in English and in Choctaw, exchanging stories as I told Lucy that this was the man who had mentored me on the long trail, acting as road builder, camp maker, raft builder, anything and everything else we had need of, including befriending whites through his fiddle playing!

Tushpatubbee, who had taken the name Johnson Bond, settled in and regaled us with his wit and storytelling as he had so often around the campfires on the trail. He reached inside his hunting coat, withdrew a stone pipe and fished out a plug of tobacco from another pocket. He reached around his belt and slowly drew out a large butcher knife.

He shaved off bits of the tobacco and filled his pipe, lighting it as he continued to speak. "I don't reckon I was favored so much by fortune when I chose to stick to the woods instead of pursuing something more substantial, but it's the kind of life I was born for."

I didn't hesitate to say, "Uncle, you have a place here as a home. Stay with us."

Lucy nodded with her gentle smile, but Tushpatubbee politely refused. "I'm a man of the woods yet and I have plenty of good years left in me. There are too many fields for hunting. They're beckoning me still. I'll set me up a place in the mountains and have all the hunting I can manage without having to cross a fence in a deer chase."

He pulled long on his pipe then nodded to the Bible always laid out somewhere in sight. This evening, it was on the mantle. "Might like to hear a bit of the Word before I go. Don't have much chance for church the way I roam."

I gladly took down the book and many happy hours were spent in reading and telling more stories before Tushpatubbee departed.

He shook my hand with a nod. "You turned out to be a fine man, Tushpa. Your folks would be pleased."

I took his praise in stride and with a humble nod. "I could do no less with what I had been given."

He left amid jovial calls of well wishes and chi pisa la chike.

A devout member of the Methodist church, I never missed a service or prayer meeting or revival. I became superintendent of the Sunday school and made the trek there no matter how inclement the weather. My family attended with me, setting a befitting example to the community. My young son, James, showed early signs of being a doer of the Word.

I struggled in revival meetings sometimes. So filled with the grace and goodness of the Spirit, my knowledge of the English language would fail me and before I knew it, I was ending my loud prayers in my mother tongue, the Chahta language. No one seemed to mind, as my zealousness caught others and many greeted me as a sincere man of God.

So I lived, a full blood Chahta Indian, son of Kanchi and Ishtoua, of Ahekutubbee on my father's side and Tekmoontubbee on my mother's side, those who possessed the noblest virtues of any man of any race.

My last request to all my sons and daughters was for them to live in the faith, as a holy legacy I wished to leave them.

This is my story, dear children. I, Tushpa or John Culberson, lived and now I die. I enjoined my son, James, to keep the family together and give them a chance for an education; to be a good citizen, and write the history of the journey if he thought it a benefit to mankind.

If my father and my mother had witnessed my life, I hope they would say, "You lived a worthy life. You pleased the Great Spirit."

Note from the Author

This story is based on a manuscript written by James Culberson, Tushpa's son. As a Choctaw, he wrote on the history and culture of his people for a number of years. Many of his writings were published in *The Chronicles of Oklahoma*. The original manuscript this story was based on is titled, "Choctaws Were Hastened in Starting Trail of Tears."

In writing *Tushpa's Story*, I struggled with other known historical facts that conflicted with the manuscript. In these instances, I often went with the manuscript. My goal with this project was to honor the original work of James Culberson.

Since this is also a work of fiction, I added characters and events to round out the story. These additions were based on actual events, characters, and legends from the time period. The story of the Arkansas Traveller became the Choctaw Traveller. The quirky Rorer was a true historical figure.

Tushpa's Story is a part of the *Touch My Tears: Tales from the Trail of Tears* collection.

Glossary of Choctaw Words

Bihi: Mulberry

Chahta: Choctaw

Chihowa: God

Chi hullo li: I love you

Chi pisa la chike: I will be seeing you, or I will see you later

Chim achukma: How are you?

Chukka: Old winter-style dwelling

Halito: A friendly greeting

Kashoffi: Forgive

Luksi: Turtle

Ome: Expressing a ready assent, agreement or acknowledgment

Yakoke: Thank you

Yakoke

This project has been on my heart to do for many years. But I wouldn't have completed it if not for the passion and dedication of those mentioned here.

Yakoke to Beverly Bringle, a direct descendant of Tushpa and James Culberson. I appreciate your open heart in endorsing this work. Having a family member's approval gave me the good conscious to publish *Tushpa's Story*. I wholeheartedly dedicate this work to you and your family.

Marilou Awiakta. Oh my. You have been such an encouraging heart behind my writing. Even in tragedy, even in difficulties, even in distance, you've been the kind voice I often needed. I will always strive to "walk in my soul" when creating stories. The threads of our lives that have woven together since I first found *Rising Fawn and the Fire Mystery* and its connection with Tushpa, is now a beautiful tapestry. I wholeheartedly dedicate this work to you as well.

Every writer needs editors, and I had two outstanding ones for this project. First editor of all my work since I was five, I give a big hug and kisses to the one who first felt my heartbeat. My mama, Lynda Kay Sawyer, told me Kanchi and Tushpa's story. We always knew we'd do something with it.

She was the encourager, researcher, first and last editor on this project. Chi hullo li. I love you.

I also want to offer a hearty yakoke to my fellow tribal member and author James Masters, who examined every character, every plot line, every sentence and every word of this manuscript, completing three layers of edits in one. Any imperfections still remaining reflect on me, not his work. Thank you, sir.

In the Historic Preservation Department of the Choctaw Nation of Oklahoma, I want to thank Ryan Spring for doing an early read of the manuscript and providing feedback. Your comments and encouraging words at the commemorative Trail of Tears Walk meant a tremendous amount to us. Yakoke!

Special thanks to Daniel Littlefield and his work with the American Native Press Archives and Sequoyah Research Center. Their online posting of the full manuscript written by James Culberson started this project.

Matthew Bradley, thank you for the comments on the early chapters of the manuscript. They encouraged and challenged me, both good things in the development of a story.

Thank you to graphic designer Kirk DouPonce with DogEared Design, and to my mama who came up with the idea for a cover that reflects the harsh journey of this story. Thanks, Kirk, for taking on this project with passion, bringing it all together. (www.DogEaredDesign.com)

A big yakoke to First Peoples Fund for financially supporting this project through my Artist in Business Leadership Fellowship. Their program has made the difference.

The greatest thanks and glory goes to our great God, Chihowa. I'm eternally grateful that He hears the prayers of my heart.

About The Author

SARAH ELISABETH SAWYER is an award-winning inspirational author, speaker and Choctaw storyteller of traditional and fictional tales based on the lives of her people. The Smithsonian's National Museum of the American Indian has honored her as a literary artist through their Artist Leadership Program for her work in preserving Trail of Tears stories.

In 2015, First Peoples Fund awarded her an Artist in Business Leadership Fellowship.

She writes from her hometown in Texas, partnering with her mama, Lynda Kay Sawyer, in continued research for future novels. Learn more about their work in preserving Choctaw history at:

SarahElisabethWrites.com (Join her newsletter for free fiction)

Facebook.com/SarahElisabethSawyer

Also By Sarah Elisabeth Sawyer

For this collection of short stories, Choctaw authors from five U.S. states came together to present a part of their ancestors' journeys, a way to honor those who walked the trail for their future. These stories not only capture a history and a culture, but the spirit, faith, and resilience of the Choctaw people.

Tears of sadness. Tears of joy. Touch and experience them.

Touch My Tears is available on Amazon.com

Choctaw Tribune Series, Book 1

Who would show up for their own execution?

It's 1892, Indian Territory. A war is brewing in the Choctaw Nation as two political parties fight out issues of old and new ways. Caught in the middle is eighteen-year-old Ruth Ann, a Choctaw who doesn't want to see her family killed.

In a small but booming pre-statehood town, her mixed blood family owns a controversial newspaper, the *Choctaw Tribune*. Ruth Ann wants to help spread the word about critical issues but there is danger for a female reporter on all fronts—socially, politically, even physically.

But what is truly worth dying for? This quest leads Ruth Ann and her brother Matthew, the stubborn editor of the fledgling *Choctaw Tribune*, to old Choctaw ways at the farm of a condemned murderer. It also brings them to head on clashes with leading townsmen who want their reports silenced no matter what.

More killings are ahead. Who will survive to know the truth? Will truth survive?

***The Executions* (Choctaw Tribune Series, Book 1) is available on Amazon.com**

With the gift to find real meaning in a story, author Sarah Elisabeth Sawyer creates tales to stir the heart and evoke deep, often buried emotions. Not one to shy away from tragedy or crisis of faith, she explores human conditions through engaging short stories.

Third Side of the Coin **is available on Amazon.com**